Elliot

and the Pixie Plot

JENNIFER A. NIELSEN

ILLUSTRATED BY GIDEON KENDALL

sourcebooks
jabberwocky

Published by Sourcebooks Jabberwocky, an imprint of Sourcebooks, Inc.
P.O. Box 4410, Naperville, Illinois 60567-4410
(630) 961-3900
Fax: (630) 961-2168
www.jabberwockykids.com

Library of Congress Cataloging-in-Publication data is on file with the publisher.

Source of Production: Sheridan Books, Chelsea, Michigan, USA
Date of Production: July 2011
Run Number: 14716

Printed and bound in the United States of America.
SB 10 9 8 7 6 5 4 3 2 1

For Sierra, who amazes me every single day.

No Pixies were harmed in the writing of this book. Sadly, we cannot say the same for our Shapeshifter, who badly stubbed his toe during the writing of chapter 7.

Contents

An entire floor of St. Phobics Hospital for Really Scared Children has been set aside just for readers of this book. If you are about to begin reading, then you may wish to take a minute first and reserve yourself a bed there. St. Phobics Hospital is located right on the Strip in Las Vegas, one of the brightest places on earth. You may not understand why that's important now, but somewhere in chapter 18 you will.

As you read, you may begin to understand myctophobia (mic-to-fo-be-a), or the fear of darkness. However, do not expect this book to help you with arachibutyrophobia (a-rak-i-something-be-a), the fear of peanut butter sticking to the roof of your mouth. There is no peanut butter in this book. Elliot's family is out of peanut butter and probably won't buy any for another month. Nor does this book deal in any way with zemmiphobia (just show the word to your teacher and she'll pronounce it for you), the fear of the great mole rat, although most readers will agree that great mole rats are pretty freaky.

If you can't get yourself to St. Phobics Hospital, then there are things you can do at home to protect yourself. First, get every lamp, flashlight, and lantern you can find, and drag them into your bedroom. Next, turn them all on. Not bright enough? Before we go any further, it is very important, no matter how afraid you are of the dark, that you never, ever light a fire in your bedroom to try to make it brighter. A fire won't give you that much more light, and it will probably burn your house down. A much better idea is to go to a baseball field and ask the owners if you can borrow all of their field lights for your bedroom. You'll need them until you're certain there is nothing in the dark that is going to try to kill you.

At least that's what Elliot wishes he had done.

Where Elliot Is Hunted

Deep inside, even past his intestines and kidneys and all that yucky stuff, eleven-year-old Elliot Penster wondered if there was something different about him. Like, maybe he was really a magical half-breed or a young wizard.

Usually in these stories, when a kid wonders about things like that, it's because he's right; that's who he is.

But that's not who Elliot is. He can wonder about it until his face turns purple, but it won't matter. The fact is he's just a regular kid.

A kid who happens to be king of the Brownies.

The story of how Elliot became king of the Brownies is pretty good. Some people think it should be in a book or something. The book could be called *Elliot and the Goblin War*, and it would probably be terrific. As a strange coincidence, a book with exactly that title does exist. Maybe it was sitting on the shelf right beside this book. But if you haven't read it, don't worry. Neither has Elliot.

All that's important to know is that he did become the Brownie king. And although it would be nice to tell you more about that now, Elliot happens to be in a bit of trouble, which requires your immediate attention.

For Elliot is being chased. *Hunted* may be a better word, because the hunter is sly and tricky and finally has Elliot square in her sights. She watched for him all week, the way a hungry lion waits in the brush for the antelope to pass by. It stops at the edge of the water hole for a drink. The lion creeps forward, and BAMMO! The antelope is captured.

Now, don't worry. That didn't happen to Elliot, mostly because he never drinks from strange water holes, and there are no lions in his small town of Sprite's Hollow. But something was waiting for him to pass by. The hunter searched everywhere for him at school, sort of like the way your little brother searches your room when he knows you've got candy hidden in there. She looked for him beneath the slide on the playground and under his desk in the classroom. Rumor is she even went into the boys bathroom to search for him. She found Elliot's twin brothers in there, shooting spit wads onto the ceiling, but no Elliot.

Then, just when Elliot thought it was safe to come out of

hiding and hurry home, the hunter spotted him. He only made it halfway home before she threw her weapon of choice, an old jump rope, around his legs and toppled him to the ground.

Elliot rolled onto his back and looked into the leering face of the scariest thing ever to cross his path—Goblins included. She was the curse of the entire fifth-grade class, the plague of Sprite's Hollow, and if the entire planet ever imploded inside a black hole, he knew that somehow she'd have caused it. The hunter, whose real name was Cambria Dawn Wortson, had found him at last.

She leaned over him with her hands on her hips. "Elliot, we have to talk."

"Later. For once, my sister isn't cooking tonight, so this might be my only chance to eat real food all month."

"Always thinking about yourself. Did you ever think that my grade is going to be ruined if we don't do our project?"

He hadn't. Elliot tried very hard never to think about anything related to Cambria Dawn Wortson. Everyone except her mother called her Cami. Elliot preferred his own nickname for her: Toadface. He had called her that once at lunch. She dumped her tray on his head and convinced the lunch lady it was an accident. Now he called her Cami too. Seemed like a good compromise.

She leaned even further over him, and he wondered how she kept her balance. In a bossy voice, she said, "Science fair projects are due next week. You didn't ask to be my partner, and I definitely didn't ask to be yours, but we're stuck with each other, so let's make the best of it, okay?"

As proof that the entire will of the universe was now focused on the single purpose of destroying Elliot's life, Cami had been assigned as his science project partner. Elliot thought back to when he had nearly been scared to death by the Goblins. If he'd known then that he would have to do a whole science project with Cami, he might have let the Goblins finish the job.

Not really. But he definitely would've moved to a different country.

"Elliot, are you listening to me?"

He was now. The way Cami pronounced his name, the last part rhymed with "Scott." Whatever. Her name rhymed with "Fanny." Almost.

"I said, are you listening?"

"Sure." He began loosening the rope around his legs. "We have to do our science project."

She huffed. Being a toadface, it was no surprise her breath smelled like a toad's. Although to be fair, he'd never really smelled toad breath before, so it was really just his best guess.

"So do you have any ideas?" she asked.

Anti-girl spray? Probably best not to suggest that, so he shrugged. Something fast and easy. That was all he cared about.

Cami plunked down beside him and pulled a notebook out from her backpack. A pink pen was lodged in the middle of it, and she opened the notebook to that page, showing him a bunch of writing that was so *girly*. The dots over her *i*'s were tiny hearts, for Pete's sake.

"Then we'll have to use my idea," she said. "I read on the Internet about a potion we can make that might turn things invisible."

Elliot snorted. That was close to the stupidest thing he'd ever heard. The actual stupidest thing was when Tubs Lawless, a boy who used to bully Elliot, had forgotten his own name. Cami gave Elliot a dirty look, then continued. "Anyway, my mom got us all the stuff, and I've already mixed it together, but she doesn't want to store it at our house in case it blows up. I figure your house already blew up once, so if it happens again it's probably not as big a deal. Okay?"

"Do I have to do anything but store it?"

"Well, it wouldn't kill you to stir it once in a while—unless stirring makes it blow up, in which case it really would kill you. My mom thinks it's probably safe just to keep it somewhere. It has to sit for a while before it can be tested. So what about it? Can I bring it over tomorrow morning?"

Tomorrow was a Saturday. Elliot had always liked the idea of never having to see Cami on the weekends, but for once in her life she was right. The project was due really soon, and if all he had to do was store it, then that didn't sound so bad.

"Fine," he said. "We'll try to turn something invisible. You can bring the potion over in the morning."

She jumped to her feet and offered him a hand up, which he ignored. She kicked her foot on the sidewalk a couple of times, then said, "By the way, I hear you finally stood up to Tubs."

"Oh, yeah." Tubs had bullied Elliot for as far back as either of them could remember. Tubs probably only remembered as far back as last week, but Elliot remembered his preschool years when Tubs used to tie Elliot to the merry-go-round with his blankie and start it spinning. After he won the Goblin war a few weeks ago, Elliot had told Tubs the bullying was going to stop. Tubs had pretty much left him alone since then. In fact, Tubs's parents had even asked if he could sleep over at Elliot's house tonight while they were out of town.

Proof that good deeds do get punished.

Cami shrugged. "Well, I thought it was really brave of you to do that. See you tomorrow!"

She skipped off down the sidewalk away from him, like the tricky hunter he knew she was. All of that being nice to him—it was just her game, her bait to draw him in. But it wouldn't work, because he was no ordinary kid. He was

Elliot Penster, king of the Brownies. And he had to hurry home before his dinner was all gone.

"Pssst, Your Highness!"

Elliot jumped back on the sidewalk as his Brownie friend Mr. Willimaker motioned to him from behind a tree. "Oh, it's you. I wondered when I'd see you again."

Mr. Willimaker pressed his bushy gray eyebrows together. "It hasn't been that long, has it?"

"Just a few weeks, I guess—since the Brownies finished rebuilding my family's blown-up house."

Mr. Willimaker nodded as if he had no clue what Elliot was talking about. "Er, yes, naturally I know all about that story, so let's say nothing more of it. I've got to talk to you. It's an emergency."

Elliot sighed and tilted his head in the direction of his home. If he really concentrated, he could almost smell his mother's lasagna from here. And he had the sinking feeling that whatever Mr. Willimaker's emergency was, it meant Elliot might not get any of her delicious dinner.

"Okay," Elliot said, sighing. "Tell me your problem."

Chapter 2

Where Elliot Meets a Triple Scoop of Evil with a Cherry on Top

Elliot followed Mr. Willimaker deeper into the orchard where he'd been hiding. "If you can be invisible to other people, then why do we have to go so far away to talk?" Elliot asked.

Mr. Willimaker frowned. "*I* can talk, but you'll look pretty silly talking back to me. You can only talk to invisible people a few times before people start to wonder about you."

"People already wonder about me." Elliot noticed something new about his friend. "Hey, you've got a white patch of hair on the back of your head. When did that happen?"

"It's always been there. You just didn't notice it," Mr. Willimaker said.

Elliot was sure he would have noticed it, but it didn't seem important to push the matter. So he set his backpack down and knelt on the ground beside Mr. Willimaker. "So what's the problem? Are the Brownies okay?"

"Probably. But we need to talk about Grissel."

Elliot's eyes narrowed. "What about him?"

Elliot wasn't the type of kid to hold grudges, but it was hard to forget that as leader of the Goblins, Grissel had scared Elliot half to death and blown up his house. Elliot finally tricked the Goblins into ending the war and eating things for dinner other than the Brownies. All of the Goblins agreed and have lived quite happily with the Brownies ever since. All of the Goblins, that is, but one.

Their leader, Grissel, is cruel and calculating and entirely unpleasant, and that's when he's in a good mood. He is not in a good mood now. That's because in addition to having lost the war, Elliot also sentenced him to hard time in the Brownie prison.

Doing hard time with the Brownies means eating chocolate cake at every meal without frosting or even a glass of milk. You'd be entirely unpleasant too if you had to eat chocolate cake day after day while surrounded by a bunch of Brownies.

"What's the problem with Grissel?" Elliot asked.

Mr. Willimaker clasped his hands together. "It's, uh, just not working out with him. I feel—er, we Brownies feel it's time to release him. We're sure he'll return peacefully to Flog and never bother anyone again."

"Did he promise that?"

Mr. Willimaker's mouth, which he must have opened to speak, dropped a little wider. "I don't, er, think we need to worry about any promises. Just give the order to release him, Elliot, right here and now, and then he can go free and we'll all return to our happy lives."

Elliot scratched his chin. "Are you all right?"

"What? Yes, of course." Mr. Willimaker tilted his head. "Why do you ask? Don't I seem like my normal self?"

"You're acting really strange."

"Ah, well, this is just how I act when I want you to release a prisoner. You've never seen me act this way, because I've never asked you to release one before."

"Oh. Well, I'm not going to release Grissel."

"What?" Mr. Willimaker threw up his hands in disbelief. "Why not?"

"Because he'll just start eating the Brownies again. Until he promises to stop, he has to stay in jail."

Mr. Willimaker's face darkened. Normally, he was excessively polite, and his tidy gray hair and suit made him look like a gentleman. But something about him was different now, and Elliot was sure he heard an angry growl escape his lips. "But Your Highness," he said between clenched teeth. "If you knew how important this is."

Elliot sat flat on the ground and rested his arms across his legs. "What's going on, Mr. Willimaker?"

Mr. Willimaker's nose began to quiver. Not his entire face. Just the nose. For a brief second it popped out like a long, pink carrot, then he took a deep breath and it flattened itself back to its regular button shape. He said, "I'm asking you for the last time, Your Highness, to release Grissel the Goblin."

Elliot stood. He placed his hands on his hips and then thought maybe that was too much like what Cami had done, so he put his hands to his side. "Who are you? Because you're not Mr. Willimaker."

The creature who was not Mr. Willimaker stared at Elliot with wide eyes while he searched for something to say. He stuttered out a few halfhearted protests, then finally leaned his head back and closed his eyes. He exhaled slowly, and as he did, the body of Mr. Willimaker dissolved, leaving in its place a small white goat.

Elliot stepped back, just to be cautious. Although he had figured whoever this was would give up trying to look like Mr. Willimaker, this was not what he had expected.

With black eyes, the goat looked up at Elliot, bleated loudly, then said, "Release Grissel or else!"

"Or else what?" Elliot asked. "What are you going to do, eat my shirt?"

"I might."

Elliot sighed and picked up his backpack. "If this is the best you can do, then I've got to go."

The goat drew in a large breath of air that seemed to fill its entire body. It stretched and expanded until it was four feet taller than Elliot. The goat's thin white hair turned dark and wild (except for a small patch of white hair on the back of its head). Long, muscular legs formed, leading to a wide, hunched back and the face of a wolf.

With a growl, the creature said, "So you're not afraid of farm animals. What about a werewolf?"

Elliot wondered why the creature hadn't turned into a werewolf to begin with. Goats don't have fangs, or sharp claws. This was much more impressive. In a bad way.

Elliot tried to keep his voice from shaking as he said, "You won't hurt me. I'll bet you're not as bad as you say you are."

"I'll take that bet," the werewolf said. "And I'll win, because I am very bad. I'm like a triple scoop of evil with a cherry on top. A wicked, evil cherry that you'll probably choke on if you don't chew carefully before swallowing."

Elliot tilted his head. "Huh?"

The werewolf leaned in closer. "I'm so evil that my

analogies don't even have to make sense. So I win the bet. Never trust anything that can change its shape."

Elliot shrugged. "In my world, the only thing I can think of that changes is a butterfly. It starts as a caterpillar, and then it changes to a butterfly. I trust butterflies. They'd never hurt me. I don't think you would either."

The werewolf raised a claw and growled so loudly that the branches of the tree behind Elliot trembled. Elliot stumbled a few steps backward and said, "Look, if you want to talk to me, then just do it as yourself."

"There is no myself," the werewolf said. "I am a Shapeshifter. I am whatever form I take at the moment."

"So this is your scary form?" Elliot asked.

The werewolf laughed, which sounded more like a pre-hunt howl. Then he asked, "Do you want to be scared?"

Elliot didn't, but it was clearly a rhetorical question. The werewolf wasn't looking for an answer. It retreated into the shadow of a tree and took a deep breath; then its height shrunk by a foot or two. The werewolf's fur blackened to become more like a body of smoke and fire than of flesh and bones. Elliot could feel the heat from the black fire, but there was no light, just the bitter smell of burning. A long, black cloak hung around the creature's shoulders, and when Elliot glanced down, he saw that the creature was only barely touching the ground.

The creature's voice was like a whisper Elliot heard in his head, but not through his ears. It ran a shiver up Elliot's spine as the creature said, "Now I am a Shadow Man. I am your worst nightmare."

Where Harold Is Also the Name of the Class Hamster

Dear Reader, this may be a good time to think about your worst nightmare. Is it one where you are being chased down a very steep hill by a million hungry white bunny rabbits and you are holding what appears to be the last carrot on earth? Or am I the only one having that dream?

Elliot doesn't remember most of his dreams. However, he felt that if he had dreamt of his Brownie friend turning into a goat, changing to a werewolf, evolving into a Shadow Man, and threatening to do something horrible to him if he didn't release Grissel, who would then turn around and do something horrible to the Brownies, he would certainly remember such a dream. So this was probably not his *worst* nightmare.

It was a pretty scary daymare though, if such a thing existed.

The Shadow Man stared down at Elliot, who felt beads of

hot sweat line his forehead. Something inside Elliot stopped working. Something important, like his heart. This was nothing like being scared to death by the Goblins. It was worse. He stumbled backward, tripping on a root and falling to the ground.

"Is this what you are?" Elliot asked, not sure what he was seeing.

The creature's laugh sounded like the powerful hiss of a steam engine pulling into a train station. "Shadow Men are servants of the evil Demon Kovol. Fear them, Elliot, and hope you never cross their path."

Elliot's heart pounded in his chest. Kovol was asleep. His friend Agatha the Hag had told him that. As long as Kovol remained asleep, the Shadow Men would have no reason to bother him. He hoped.

"You're not Mr. Willimaker, and you're not a goat or a werewolf," Elliot whispered. "And you can take the shape of a Shadow Man, but that's not you either."

"I am far more powerful than they are, for I can become them when I want to, or become anything else. I am a Shapeshifter, and you will do what I say."

Elliot shook his head and forced himself to look into the empty black pits that were now the Shapeshifter's eyes. "You're made of shadow. You can't hurt me."

The figure swirled around Elliot, creating a wind that

sucked the air from his lungs. Heat from the Shadow Man filled the space where the air had been, and sweat stung Elliot's brow. He collapsed forward and whispered, "Okay, I get it. You're bad."

The swirling stopped, and Elliot was able to breathe again. "I'm not bad actually," the Shapeshifter said. "I just wanted to scare you because you bet me I couldn't."

"You win, okay? Please change."

The Shadow Man shrugged as if it didn't matter to him, then exhaled slowly and dissolved into the shape of a boy about Elliot's age.

The boy was about Elliot's height but with normal legs (Elliot's legs were still too long for his body). Elliot's hair had darkened since summer to the same light brown as the boy's, although streaks of blond still showed in Elliot's sun-bleached hair. And unlike Elliot, the boy's clothes matched. Elliot wondered if he'd change anything about his own body if he were a Shapeshifter. Bigger muscles maybe.

"What's your name?" Elliot asked.

"Harold."

"Harold?"

"All the best Shapeshifter names were taken before I was born. By the time I came along, it was either Morphid or Pupa Boy." He shrugged. "My parents skipped Shapeshifter names and called me Harold instead."

"Harold's good. That's our hamster's name at school."

Harold groaned. "That doesn't make me feel better."

"It should. He's a good hamster. Runs fast on his wheel and everything. I guess you already know my name."

"Obviously. Now please, King Elliot, you must release Grissel."

"Why?"

"All I know is that the Pixies want him free. They forced me to come here and try to fool you into releasing them."

"How did they force you?"

Harold threw up his hands. "How many times has your mother told you that rhyme, 'Pixie one, lots of fun. Pixie two, trouble for you. Pixie three, better flee.'"

"Never." Elliot's mother didn't know Pixies exist.

"Well, my mother says it every time the Pixies trick me. She says it a lot. Anyway, they said I wasn't a very good Shapeshifter, because I couldn't turn into anything I wanted. I said I could. They bet me I couldn't." Harold lowered his eyes. "I have this problem with bets. I can't say no to them."

"What did they want you to turn into?" Elliot asked.

Harold's mouth twisted. Then with a sigh he said, "A marshmallow."

Elliot giggled. "Regular or mini?"

"It's not funny," Harold said. "Of course I had to prove that I could do it. Then when I became a marshmallow I couldn't think my way back, because as it turns out, marshmallows

don't have brains. The Pixies said they'd change me back but that I had to do what they wanted."

"What was that?"

"They wanted me to pretend to be you and order the Brownies to release Grissel. But even if I looked exactly like you, I still wouldn't be the king, so I couldn't release him. So after they helped me change back, I promised that if they released me, I'd come here pretending to be Mr. Willimaker. The Pixie princess, Fidget Spitfly, agreed, and here I am. So will you release Grissel?"

Elliot wasn't usually a stubborn kid, but he didn't see a lot of room to bargain on the issue of Goblins eating his royal subjects. "You'll have to go back and tell Princess Fidget that I'm not releasing Grissel until he promises to stop eating the Brownies."

Harold shook his head. "Are you crazy? I'm not telling her anything. Do you know how mad she'll be that I failed? Sorry, but you'll have to tell her yourself."

"If she comes after me, I'll just capture her," Elliot said. If he had done that with the Goblins, he could surely do that with her.

"She's not some stupid Goblin, Elliot. When Princess Fidget wants you, you'll be the one coming to her."

Elliot didn't like the sound of that. "How? When?"

"I don't know. But if I were you, I wouldn't go to sleep."

"Tonight?"

"Ever." With that, Harold exhaled slowly, and his human body dissolved into the shape of a brown sparrow. He fluttered into the air, waved a wing at Elliot, and then began to fly away. He circled around and stopped midair in front of Elliot, then tweeted, "Sorry about trying to trick you."

"That's okay," Elliot said.

"Maybe I can make it up to you in some way."

"Yeah, maybe."

"Penster!"

Elliot rolled his eyes and turned. Crashing through the bushes was Tubs Lawless, his least favorite former bully.

"Okay, Penster, now you're going to have to deal with me!"

Chapter 4

Where Elliot Has Other Things on His Mind

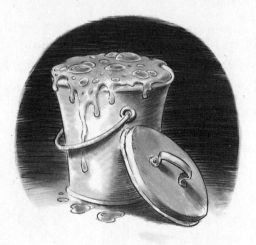

Not so long ago, if Tubs Lawless had crashed through the bushes and told Elliot, "Now you're going to have to deal with me," what that really would have meant is, "Now you're going to have to deal with a twisted neck." These days what he meant probably wasn't a whole lot better. It meant Elliot would have to deal with Tubs through an entire sleepover that night.

"My stuff's already at your house," Tubs said. "My parents dropped it off before they went out of town. I already ate the rest of your mom's lasagna, because I'm always hungry after school. Wendy said she'd cook you something to eat if you ever decide to come home from school."

"More like she'll burn me something to eat," Elliot said grimly. Maybe he could have real food next year.

"Anyway, I told her that I'd find you and drag you back home."

"I know the way to my own house. I was just talking to someone."

"I saw that. You were talking to a bird." Tubs gave Elliot what was probably meant to be a playful jab in the arm. Elliot wondered if it would leave a bruise. "Who are you, Snow White or something?"

Elliot nodded and slung his backpack over his shoulder. "Yeah, something like that."

Tubs pretty much stopped talking at that point, which was fine by Elliot, who would have preferred to be alone. He wanted to think about everything Harold had said, and what it might mean for him.

The only thing Elliot knew about Pixies was that during

the Goblin war, Fudd Fartwick had borrowed some of their magic to make Elliot's bedroom disappear. Fudd had been an advisor to the queen of the Brownies before Elliot took her place. Then Fudd had worked with the Goblins to try to get Elliot killed so that Fudd could become king.

When Elliot won the Goblin war, Fudd had confessed to his crimes and promised to change. No one had worked harder in getting Elliot's blown-up house rebuilt than Fudd Fartwick. He even made it so that the stairway didn't squeak anymore.

If Tubs weren't walking beside him now, Elliot would have called for Fudd to come talk to him and tell him everything he knew about the Pixies and their princess, Fidget Spitfly.

But Tubs had started talking again. Elliot wasn't paying much attention, but it sounded like a story about Tubs last Halloween.

"My mom says I'm too old for trick-or-treating," Tubs was saying, "but I think, who's too old for candy? Not me."

Elliot smiled. Finally he and Tubs had something in common.

Tubs continued, "Did I ever tell you about a few years ago when I saw these kids in Goblin costumes? They looked so cool, I could've sworn they were real."

Elliot shoved his hands into his pockets. "Do you think Goblins exist, then?"

Tubs snorted. "They weren't real Goblins, dork. They were eating all these pickles, and a real Goblin wouldn't eat pickles."

"Right," Elliot muttered, thinking about how the Goblins had started a whole war with the Brownies over a bag of pickles.

Elliot's mind wandered back to his own troubles. If Princess Fidget was so dangerous, why hadn't Mr. Willimaker warned Elliot about her? Mr. Willimaker had told Elliot everything he needed to know about the Goblins during the war. Why hadn't anyone told him about Pixies? Maybe Harold was making Princess Fidget sound worse than she really was. Just because he got himself tricked into becoming a marshmallow didn't mean Elliot was in any danger of being tricked. After all, Elliot couldn't turn himself into a marshmallow, even if he wanted to. Which he didn't, by the way.

He also wondered about the Shadow Men. When Harold had turned into one, everything in Elliot's body froze with fear. And that wasn't even a real Shadow Man. It was just a Shapeshifter pretending to be one. He was glad Kovol remained asleep, because he'd rather face a hundred Goblins trying to scare him to death before he faced a real Shadow Man.

"Hey, Tubs," Elliot said. "Are you afraid of anything?"

Tubs shrugged. "You'd have to be stupid not to be afraid of something."

"But you are—" Elliot stopped. It didn't seem like a good idea to point out the obvious, which was that several important pieces of Tubs's brain seemed to be missing, such as the thinking piece.

"So what are you afraid of?" Elliot asked instead.

"Same thing everyone's afraid of," Tubs said.

"Snakes?"

"No, you wimp. Afraid that the ground beneath us will suddenly turn to quicksand and all of Sprite's Hollow will be swallowed up under the world."

"Why are you talking about the Underworld?" Elliot said quickly. "There's no Underworld."

"Sure there is," Tubs said.

Elliot stopped walking. "How do you know?"

"The clouds are over the world. We're on the world. The dirt is under the world."

Elliot breathed a sigh of relief and kept walking. "Oh, yeah, sure." When he first became king, Mr. Willimaker had told Elliot that if he ever shared the secret of the Underworld with anyone, the Brownies would never be able to return to him again.

When they got home, Wendy met Elliot at the front door. "Why didn't you save me any dinner?" he scowled at her.

Wendy's eyes widened, then she said, "Mom told you to hurry home. But I can make you something else if you want."

"Nah. I can ruin my own food later on."

Wendy frowned, and Elliot knew he had hurt her feelings. But she shrugged it off and said, "You need to go to the backyard. You have a visitor."

"Who?" Elliot asked.

"Oh, just a *special* visitor who wants to see you. Better hurry."

Elliot handed her his backpack, then walked around his house into the backyard. Beyond the grass was the end of Sprite's Hollow and the beginning of a thickly wooded area that went on for miles. Since nobody had ever bothered to think of a name for it, everyone just called it "the woods." When Elliot saw who his visitor was, his eyes flicked to the woods. The idea of hiding there for a couple of years until it was safe to come out again crossed his mind.

Cami was sitting on the ground weaving blades of grass together. She was working on a chain that was now almost as long as her arm.

"Hey," he said, "stop using up all my family's grass."

"Sorry," she said, throwing the grass chain down. "I didn't realize you were down to your last gazillion blades."

"Never mind," he said. "What's going on? I thought you weren't coming here until tomorrow morning."

"Yeah, but when I got home my mom said I have a soccer game in the morning. Are you just getting home from school now? You're slow."

Elliot let Cami's comment pass and followed her to a big white bucket with a black lid on it. "I've added the ingredients already," she said. "I won't tell you everything that's in there, because you really don't want to know. The recipe says it has to sit in the sun for five days, then it's ready."

"Can I look in it?"

"Sure. Just don't smell it too deeply, because it'll probably kill brain cells."

Elliot opened the lid and immediately slammed it closed. "It smells like something died in there."

Cami nodded. "Like I said, you don't want to know about the ingredients."

Elliot cracked the lid open again. The liquid inside was clear and thick like syrup. Every now and then a thick bubble rose to the top and popped, even though it wasn't cooking. Elliot shut the lid. "So what do I have to do?"

"Nothing but let it sit. Stir it if you want." Cami began to walk away but then turned back to him. "Oh, and one more thing, if it starts making noises, then you'd better get everyone out of the house, because that means it's going to blow up."

"What kind of noises?" Elliot asked.

"I dunno," Cami said. "It's a liquid, so it probably shouldn't make any noises at all. Anyway, I'll come back in a day or two and check on it."

As she began to leave, Kyle and Cole, Elliot's six-year-old twin brothers, ran to Cami and Elliot. "Secret lovers, hiding place. Secret lovers, kissy face," they teased.

Elliot picked up a stick and hurled it toward his brothers. "Stop bothering me all the time!" he yelled, although this was in fact the first time they'd bothered him all day.

Cami shrugged. "I have to go anyway."

"You really should go out through the gate on the other side of the house," one of the twins said. It was probably Cole, Elliot thought. He had trouble telling the twins apart.

"But there's no fence in your yard," Cami said. "Why do you have a gate if there's no fence?"

"It's rude to cross the grass where there would be a fence if we had a fence. Use the gate." Kyle winked at Cole as he finished, but Elliot didn't think Cami noticed.

"All right," Cami said and followed the twins to the gate. She waved at Elliot in such a nice way that he couldn't help but wonder what devious tricks she had up her sleeve. Then he noticed she wore a short-sleeved shirt, so she probably didn't have room for any tricks up there. And if she did, they probably weren't very good tricks.

Elliot was so busy wondering about Cami's tricks, he didn't notice how watchful Kyle and Cole were being until it was too late. Kyle and Cole only watched what entertained them, and something about Cami leaving through the gate definitely had their attention.

She stepped on a pile of grass that instantly sunk beneath her feet, leaving Cami knee deep in mud.

Only a few weeks ago, Kyle and Cole had been fascinated with water. It only made sense that by now they had moved on to mud.

Cami's face turned red, the color a face gets when a person is really mad. She tried to pull her legs out but only got more mud on herself. "I'm stuck," she said to the twins. "Help me." They only laughed, which of course made her face even redder.

Elliot didn't wait around to see what happened next. He yelled, "Okay, well, I'll keep an eye on the science project for you," and ran away.

Chapter
5

Where Tubs Is a Deep Sleeper

Those readers who lived near Lake Baikal in Russia on June 30, 1908, will remember the meteor explosion that occurred a few miles up in the sky. Some 80 million trees were knocked over from the force of the explosion, and glass windows shattered as far as a hundred miles away. If there is anyone reading this story who did *not* happen to be living near Lake Baikal over a hundred years ago, then you should know it is considered to be the loudest single event ever to happen on this earth. It was a hundred times louder than a one-ton bomb and was more than three times the sound required to cause hearing loss.

Lying in his room that night, with his ears sandwiched between two pillows, Elliot was sure he had discovered the second loudest sound in history.

Tubs was snoring.

Tubs snorted in air, and Elliot thought this must be what it's like inside a tornado.

Then Tubs exhaled, and Elliot imagined a million tiny Tubs germs being sent as far away as the jungles of Africa, all riding on a single breath.

Mother had insisted that Elliot let Tubs use his bed for the night. "He doesn't have things as good as you," she told Elliot. "Be nice and let him have the bed."

Tubs could literally have his bed now, Elliot thought. He didn't think he ever wanted it back again.

When Tubs took Elliot's bed, Elliot took his older brother Reed's bed and made Reed sleep on the floor. It had seemed fair at the time, although now Elliot wasn't so sure. Reed didn't stay on the floor for long. He had finally left about an hour ago, saying he was going in to work at the Quack Shack, his fast-food duck burgers job, either on the really late night shift or on the really early morning shift, whichever was closer. Elliot rolled over in Reed's bed and tried to plug his ears with Reed's pillow.

Tubs drew in another breath. It sounded like a train running through Elliot's room.

Elliot threw off his covers and shoved his feet into a pair of slippers beside his bed. They were Reed's, but he'd only borrow them for a minute. Elliot trudged downstairs and into the kitchen to get a drink of water. Maybe he could take some of that water upstairs and throw it on Tubs. That'd get him to stop snoring.

Elliot was halfway through his glass of water when he heard heavy footsteps clomping down the stairs. Tubs must've woken up for a drink too.

"Snoring must make you thirsty," Elliot said, but as Tubs entered the kitchen he didn't answer. He didn't even really seem to be awake.

"Tubs?" Elliot asked.

"Pretty mist," Tubs mumbled, reaching out his hand.

Elliot squinted. The kitchen was dark enough that he hadn't noticed it, but in a beam of moonlight through the window, he did see what appeared to be a silver mist. His first thought was of the Shadow Men, but theirs was a dense, black smoke. This was lighter, and it was pretty in a spooky sort of way.

But what was it?

Elliot flipped on the kitchen light, and the mist sparkled to life, as though it were made of thousands of mirrors. Its shape folded and curved like a fast-moving cloud.

Elliot ran his hand through the mist, then pulled it away when it stung him. "Okay, sorry," he muttered. The mist clearly had touch issues.

It moved toward the back door with Tubs following

obediently behind. Elliot grabbed his arm, but he might as well have tried to slow down an elephant for all the good it did him. Tubs put a hand on Elliot's face and shoved him to the ground without breaking his stride.

"Tubs!" Elliot called. "What are you doing?"

"Pretty mist," Tubs said again.

Elliot thought Tubs was sleepwalking, but he couldn't be sure. Tubs said a lot of strange things while he was fully awake too.

Elliot leapt to his feet and tried to block Tubs from opening the door, but Tubs pushed past Elliot as if he were made of feathers. The mist expanded once it reached open air and continued to lure Tubs away.

"Wake up, Tubs!" Elliot cried. He considered running upstairs to get his dad's help, but Tubs would be gone before Elliot could get back. He grabbed a rock and threw it at Tubs's back. It hit with a klunk but bounced off without Tubs reacting.

Elliot was a little relieved about that. If Tubs had reacted, Elliot would have a bloody nose already.

He ran up to Tubs and began punching his arm, yelling at him to stop, and kicking at his legs. In any other situation, Elliot might have considered this a golden opportunity. But the mist was beginning to worry him. It was clearly something magical, but why did it want Tubs?

Elliot decided to appeal directly to the mist. "Hey!" he yelled. He swatted his hand through the mist, even though it felt like he was being bitten each time. "Where are you taking him?"

The mist didn't answer, which wasn't surprising considering that it had no mouth. It led Tubs across Elliot's backyard grass, all the while folding and dancing in the air. It was taking him into the woods behind Elliot's house. Elliot barely liked going there during the day. And as dark as it was out here in Elliot's yard, it was even darker in the woods.

"Wake up, Tubs!" Elliot called again. "Come back to my house. We have candy in there! Remember, you like candy!"

Tubs hesitated, just for a moment, and then continued to follow the mist.

Elliot ran back to his house and grabbed the hose that had been Kyle and Cole's favorite toy for the last several months. He turned it on full blast and shot a stream of water at Tubs, who kept walking as if unaware. So Elliot shot the water toward the mist. It created some sort of barrier that turned the water back on Elliot and soaked him with what felt like an entire lake of water splashing down on his head.

Elliot turned the hose off and sloshed back to Tubs, now at the edge of the woods. Obviously there was nothing he could do to wake Tubs up, but he could speak again to the mist.

"Whatever you are, you don't want him," Elliot yelled.

"Trust me, you really don't! Just take me instead. I'll go with you, but leave him out of this!"

"Like, you're totally in the way, human," a girl's voice said.

It didn't come from the mist. Elliot swung around and saw a bright light a little deeper into the woods, like a small star had landed there.

"Who are you?" Elliot walked toward the light. Whoever had spoken was hidden behind a row of fallen trees. He climbed over the trees, now with Tubs only a few steps behind him. In front of him was a...a...a—he didn't know exactly what.

She was a foot high and didn't look any older than he was, but she sounded like one of those teenagers who thought she was cooler than everyone else. She had round wings; long, thin ears; and a bunch of curly, yellow hair. Her dress was bright red, purple, and yellow, and looked like something a little girl would dance around in, just to watch the skirt twirl. Around her neck were several loops of the grass chain that Cami had woven in his backyard earlier that day.

"Are you a Fairy?" he asked.

The girl shot a furious look at him and aimed her wand in his direction. Instantly a tree grabbed Elliot's right leg and yanked him upside down high into the air.

"I so totally don't need to be insulted right now," she said. "If I didn't have more important things to do, I'd just hurl you into space or something."

37

Okay, she wasn't a Fairy. But how was he supposed to know?

Elliot watched the mist approach her. It swirled in a wide circle and then settled at her feet. Slowly the particles of mist revealed themselves to be other similar creatures, each one bowing to her first. They all wore brightly colored dresses too, like a rainbow had exploded all over them.

Tubs stood in front of them. His eyes were open, but he didn't appear to be seeing anything. "No more pretty mist?" he mumbled.

The not-a-Fairy who had spoken before said to the others with her, "Wow, humans are so lame-brained. Grissel should've told me."

Grissel? Was this the Pixie princess, Fidget Spitfly? He wondered if she liked to spit on flies.

And she talked funny. He knew it wasn't Flibberish, the language of the Underworld, but he didn't know any humans who talked like her either. Not even his sister Wendy's giggly friends.

Fidget stood and fluttered into the air so that she was directly in front of Tubs. "So, dude, it would be totally awesome if you released Grissel from the Brownie jail," she said, tossing her pile of curly blond hair behind her shoulders.

"Surc," Tubs mumbled, clearly still asleep. "He's released."

Above them, Elliot kept silent. Tubs had been sleeping in Elliot's bed, so they must have thought Tubs was king of the

Brownies. Elliot hoped the Pixies would think Grissel had been released and would leave long enough for him to get Tubs safely back to the house.

But it didn't happen that way. A Pixie poofed beside Fidget a moment later and whispered something in her ear. Fidget angrily sliced her wand through the air. Responding to her magic, hundreds of fall leaves lifted into the air and began swirling like a tornado around Tubs. The wind it created rushed up into Elliot's face.

"Not awesome!" she said with a shrill, high-pitched voice. "You totally tried to trick me!"

"Totally uncool," Tubs agreed.

Her voice got even higher and angrier. "You want to keep Grissel in jail? Then I'll keep *you* in jail!"

The tornado tightened around Tubs until in a flash of light he was gone.

"No!" Elliot cried. "Bring him back!"

Fidget seemed to have forgotten about Elliot until then. She fluttered up beside him, then said, "Human, you totally have to look at me so I can do this little forgetting spell on you. What you saw was just between the Pixies and Brownies. Way not any of your business."

"I'm afraid it is," Elliot said.

Her eyes narrowed. "Like, why?"

"Bring him back, and I'll tell you."

With a wave of her wand, the tree dangled Elliot higher. It had loosened its grip, and Elliot felt sure if he wiggled too much he'd go crashing to the ground. Even if his head was still attached after he fell, he would probably get one monster headache.

"That human has no power to release Grissel," Elliot said. "Only the Brownie king can do that."

Fidget's eyes darted to where Tubs had stood, then back at Elliot. "What's your name?" she asked.

"I'm Elliot Penster, king of the Brownies. I'm the one you want."

"Oh, fruit rot!" Fidget scowled. "You're the king and not him? Okay, so you heard the whole speech before. Are you going to release Grissel or not?"

"Not," Elliot said.

"What-ever." Fidget flicked her wand and the tree released Elliot. Wind blew up at him as the dark ground rushed to greet his fall. The last thing he remembered was the ground about two inches from his face.

Chapter 6

Where *Surfer Teen* Is the Awesomest

Some kids wake up to the sun shining through their bedroom windows. Others wake to an alarm clock on their bedside table. For some kids, their mother sings some annoying good-morning song while bacon sizzles on a pan in the kitchen.

Elliot Penster woke up to Tubs punching his arm.

"What?" he scowled, swatting Tubs away. "Stop that, I'm awake!"

"Where are we?" Tubs asked. "How'd we get here?"

Elliot slowly sat up and absorbed their surroundings. They were deep underground, in the Underworld obviously, and in a small cave with thick tree roots serving as the bars of their jail cell. This must be a Pixie jail.

"When you said I couldn't bully you anymore, I told myself fine, there's plenty of other kids to beat on," Tubs said. "And I haven't touched you for weeks, even when you did something so stupid that I should have beat you up at least a little. But I know that our being here is somehow your fault, Penster, and I'm going to get you for it."

"Will you be quiet?" Elliot hissed. "First we've got to get out of here, then you can beat me up."

"Yeah, but if you save us, then I'll feel bad about beating you up," Tubs said. "I'd rather do it now."

Elliot scratched his foot across the ground toward Tubs, hoping to kick dirt in his face, but he was still wearing Reed's slippers, which were soaking wet, so he only ended up smearing mud across his leg.

"I'm hungry," Tubs said. "And really, really confused."

Elliot crept to the bars, hoping to see more of where they were. The cave that trapped them seemed to be at the top of a tall hill. Far below them was what appeared to be a thick patch of woods. Bass drums beat a soft rhythm somewhere inside them, and colored sparks of light constantly jetted into the air in various places. Those woods were probably the Pixies' home.

He wondered how far away the Brownies' home of

Burrowsville was. Did they know he was here? If so, was there anything they could do to get him out?

"Mr. Willimaker," Elliot hissed. "Mr. Willimaker!" There was no other Brownie who Elliot trusted more. If anyone could help, it was Mr. Willimaker.

"What are you doing?" Tubs asked.

Elliot turned back to Tubs, who looked so relaxed leaning against the dirt wall that he might as easily have been sunbathing. "I'm working on getting us out of here," Elliot said.

"Okay, you do that, and I'll work on my thing," Tubs said.

"What's your thing?" Elliot asked.

"Taking a nap. I didn't sleep so well last night."

"That's because you were wandering all over my yard and got us here in the first place!" Elliot said.

"Yeah? Well, you should've tried to stop me," Tubs said.

Elliot scowled and turned back to the bars. "Mr. Willimaker?" he called more loudly.

He jumped away from the bars as a figure poofed in front of him. Not Mr. Willimaker, but Fidget Spitfly. Her hair was in a high ponytail on the side of her head. She had so much hair, he wondered why it didn't make her tip over sideways. She wore a bright purple dress today. Really bright and really purple. Elliot felt a headache coming on just looking at her.

"Do you really think anyone can hear you calling while

you're my prisoner?" she asked. "How clueless would I have to be if I made it that easy? As if!"

Elliot lifted his eyebrows. "Where did you learn my language? You talk...different."

"Only on the best human television show ever, *Surfer Teen*. It's so totally the awesomest show of the whole universe!"

Dear Reader, *Surfer Teen* so totally is not the awesomest show in the universe. In the first place, *awesomest* is not even a word, but the actors in *Surfer Teen* don't seem to know that, since they use the word in almost every sentence. And in the second place, the show was only on for one season, because it so totally was the stupidest show in the history of television, which is quite an accomplishment. But it is Fidget Spitfly's favorite show, and she has watched every episode at least 458 times. She has watched the episode where the awesomest boy first kisses the hottest-to-the-max girl at least 873 times. Totally.

Elliot rolled his eyes. His sister, Wendy, used to watch *Surfer Teen*. Now he felt like he was talking to one of the characters on the show. "Listen," he said to Fidget, "I'm the one you want. This other human here with me can't do anything for you. Send him home, and then you and I can talk."

"Just wait one minute," Tubs said, getting to his feet. "Let me understand something first. Am I having the weirdest dream ever or not?" Then he punched himself in the eye. "Ow! I hate it when I do that."

"Why did you?" Elliot asked.

Tubs glared at him. "It proved that I'm awake, didn't it?"

"You are awake," Elliot said. "We're being held by the Pixies in the Underworld."

"Oh," Tubs said, as if that sort of thing happened all the time.

Fidget eyed Tubs, who was now busy picking his nose. "I'm just hungry," Tubs muttered. "My parents are out of town anyway, so if you get me something to eat, I don't care if you send me back or not."

Fidget smiled and said to Tubs, "Like, get your friend to release Grissel, and I'll give you anything to eat that you want."

"Anything?" Tubs asked. At the moment, all he had to eat was whatever he'd pulled from his nose, so he seemed to like this idea. "Anything, like a big bowl of hot fudge topping for breakfast?"

"Totally," Fidget whispered.

Tubs grabbed Elliot by the neck and shoved his face into the tree root bars. "Tell her you'll do what she wants, jerk."

Elliot kicked his foot out behind him and sank it into Tubs's chubby stomach. Tubs released him with a gasp, and Elliot fell to the ground. He rubbed his neck, then said to Fidget, "Before I can do anything, I have to talk to Mr. Willimaker. If I can't call him, then will you send someone to let him know I'm here?"

"You can't call him," Fidget said, "but I can."

She flicked her wand, and immediately Mr. Willimaker appeared beside her. Unfortunately, he seemed to be just getting out of his bath. He had a towel around his waist, and his gray hair was still wet and sticking up in all directions. Most Brownies liked the just-stepped-out-of-a-tornado look, but Mr. Willimaker always tried to keep his hair neatly combed.

"Another Pixie?" Tubs asked.

"Brownie," Elliot said.

"He looks like a gopher with hands," Tubs whispered. Luckily, Mr. Willimaker was so confused, Elliot didn't think he heard.

"What—" Mr. Willimaker gasped, then he saw Elliot. "Oh, Your Highness." He tightened the towel around himself and then turned to Fidget. "Princess Fidget, I demand an explanation."

"Like, chill out," she said. "You release Grissel, and I'll let you have your king back."

"Elliot's a king? But he's such a dork!" Tubs started laughing so hard that tears rolled down his face.

"He happens to be a very good king," Mr. Willimaker said. Then to Fidget, he added, "You know I can't release him without King Elliot's orders."

"Duh! So make him give the order."

"I won't," Elliot said.

"Is there someplace he and I can talk?" Mr. Willimaker asked Fidget. "Somewhere private?"

Fidget waved her wand again. In an instant, Elliot and Mr. Willimaker found themselves perched at the top of a lofty tree. They were so high up that Elliot couldn't see the ground. He only assumed it was somewhere far down below him. He grabbed the branch beneath him and held on tightly. Mr. Willimaker seemed more concerned about keeping his towel wrapped around himself than with falling.

"I'm so sorry, Your Highness," Mr. Willimaker began. "I knew she was talking to Grissel in the prison, but I didn't know they were planning something like this."

"Grissel never said anything?"

"A few days ago Grissel told his guards that the Pixies were forming a plot for his escape. I just didn't know it would be something like *this*."

Elliot rolled his eyes. "And you didn't think you should've told me about that?"

"Yes, obviously I should have told you. Forgive me."

"It's too late to worry about that now. Can you help me escape?"

"Pixie magic is more powerful than mine. I can't stop her from keeping you here." He twisted his hands together. "What are we going to do?"

Elliot grabbed Mr. Willimaker's hands and untwisted

them, then said, "I'll figure a way out of this mess, but I'm not going to release Grissel."

"I think you have to, Your Highness."

"Why?"

Mr. Willimaker looked up at Elliot with a frown. "If you don't, she'll kill you."

Chapter 7

Where Harold Offers
the Worst Kind of Help

M r. Willimaker finally left Elliot with the agreement that he would speak to Grissel to find out what he knew about the Pixies' plot. As soon as Mr. Willimaker poofed away, Elliot was poofed back into the jail. Princess Fidget wasn't there anymore. In her place was another Pixie girl, also with blond hair but with bright blue eyes.

"Who are you?" Elliot asked.

"Claire. Princess Fidget's advisor. She asked me to tell you that she is 'so totally tired of waiting around' that I could 'gag her with a spoon.'"

Elliot smiled. "So did you?"

"What?"

"Gag her with a spoon?"

Claire shook her head. "There's a pretty strict no-gagging-the-princess-with-a-spoon rule here. Even when she deserves it."

Elliot glanced behind him where Tubs was sleeping peacefully, his thumb in his mouth.

"What'd you do to him?" Elliot asked.

"Nothing," Claire said. "He just got tired of waiting too. He said his brain hurt from trying to figure everything out." Claire used a tiny hand to push some hair off her forehead, revealing a thin streak of white hair underneath the rest.

"You don't talk like the princess," Elliot said, eyeing the Pixie suspiciously.

"I bet you think all Pixies talk the same," Claire said. "Wanna bet they don't?"

Elliot stared carefully at Claire. "Harold, is that you?"

Harold the Pixie looked around to be sure nobody else was there and then flew in closer to Elliot. "I don't have long, but I wanted to come see you. Because if you really think about it, this could be a little bit my fault."

"A little bit?"

"Okay, a lot. I feel guilty. But I'll try to help you now."

Elliot pushed at the tree root bars of the jail. "Can you get me out of here?"

"I can imitate the Pixie look, but not their magic. Elliot, you have to release Grissel."

"Why does Fidget want Grissel released anyway? Are they friends?"

"As Fidget would say, 'That's so grody.' No, you've heard of the Totally Tubular Turf War, right?"

Elliot shook his head.

Harold folded his short Pixie arms. "I don't mean to lecture, because I'll only sound like my mother, but if you're going to be king of the Brownies, you should at least take ten minutes to learn about the Underworld."

"Sorry," Elliot said. "I've been busy with this science fair project."

Claire—or Harold—continued. "Ever since creatures entered the Underworld, Fairies and Pixies have battled over the land known as the Glimmering Forest. Woodland is hard to find down here, and this is the best in all the Underworld. Streams and rivers flow from beautiful waterfalls. Flowers of every color and variety grow wild. And the trees live forever in the Glimmering Forest."

"Sounds nice," Elliot said.

"Nice? That's like saying turnip juice is only pretty good. The Fairies want Glimmering Forest, and the Pixies want it too, but neither of them will share the land. Grissel promised Fidget that if she gets him free from Brownie prison, he'll blow up all the Fairy settlements that border the Glimmering Forest. Then the Pixies think they can take the rest of the forest for themselves."

"I can't help Fidget get a bunch of Fairies hurt. Do her parents know about this?"

"The king and queen of the Pixies are on vacation. They told Fidget if she solved the Fairy problem before they came back, they'd let her take surfing lessons."

"Mr. Willimaker says that if I don't release Grissel, the Pixies will kill me," Elliot said.

"Probably." Harold fluttered down on a rock and rested his head on his hands. "I love flying, but it's tiring."

"Can we get back to fixing my problem?" Elliot asked.

"Huh? Oh, I can't fix your problem. I'm a Shapeshifter, not a miracle maker. But I can do one thing for you. It'll be morning soon at your house. Until you get this all worked out, I'll go to the surface and pretend to be you."

"No thanks," Elliot said.

"It'll be fine," Harold said. "I've imitated humans plenty of times before. No one will even notice a difference."

"Don't," Elliot said.

"You'd rather your mom wakes up and finds you missing?"

"My family might not care. I wasn't very nice to them before I left."

Harold grabbed a root to get closer to Elliot in his jail. "You want the whole town of Sprite's Hollow out looking for you, your picture in the paper? All that homework you'd miss?"

Elliot sighed. "Okay, fine. But you can't change things or do anything different from what I would do. Just stay in my room as much as you can, and don't talk to anyone unless you have to."

"No problem," Harold said.

Elliot gestured at Tubs, who was still sleeping. "What about him?"

Harold shrugged. "I already put his clothes over a bucket and mop in the corner of your kitchen. So far nobody's noticed that it's not him. Just do what the Pixies want, and you'll both be home soon."

With that, Harold snapped his fingers and poofed away. Tubs was taking up the entire space on the ground of their cell, so there was no room to sit. Elliot leaned against the wall at the edge of the jail and closed his eyes to think. He didn't know what worried him most—that the Pixies were going to kill him, or that Harold the Shapeshifter was going to take his place at home.

Where Elliot Wants a Time-Out

Dear Reader, in this chapter, you're going to hear about Elliot's next visitor to his jail. You may wonder if his next visitor is Diffle McSnug, who has recently returned from an exciting trip to the Far East, where his hot air balloon became tangled in a flock of migrating geese. Of course, as you should well know, there is no character in this book named Diffle McSnug. Don't you think Elliot would be confused if a character who doesn't exist in this book suddenly showed up at his Pixie prison with a story about hot air balloons and migrating geese? It's too bad Diffle's not a character, though. You would bite off your fingernails with fright hearing how Diffle fell to the earth after the angry geese chewed through the ropes of his basket. And you'd be shocked to know the amazing way he survived. You wouldn't believe it, even if you heard the story.

Which of course, you won't, because this is Elliot's story. Diffle needs to get his own book.

Elliot only had to wait about twenty minutes before his next visitor (not Diffle McSnug) poofed in to see him.

Mr. Willimaker's daughter, Patches, ran forward, trying to hug Elliot through the thick tree root bars of his prison. This really meant that she hugged the bars more than she hugged Elliot, but, Dear Reader, you should not take this to mean that Patches loved the prison more than she loved Elliot. She just couldn't reach him, that's all.

Elliot had saved Patches from the Goblins twice. In her opinion, that made Elliot at least as cool as her great-great grandfather Willimaker, who had fought in the Demon wars a thousand years ago.

"Here," she said, pushing a wrapped-up bundle to Elliot.

"What's this?" he asked.

"Food. Carrots and beets and some turnip juice. And a couple of pickles."

Elliot already knew about the pickles. Pickle juice was leaking from the bundle onto his brother Reed's slippers, which were pretty much ruined by now.

"Thanks," Elliot said, although ever since he'd learned the Pixies planned to kill him, he hadn't felt very hungry, not even for pickles. He set the bundle on the ground for when Tubs woke up. Tubs would be hungry no matter who wanted to kill him. Elliot had once seen Tubs so hungry at the Quack Shack that he ate his entire duck burger without taking the paper wrapping off it first. And rumor had it that Tubs had once buttered his lunch tray at school. He'd broken off a tooth trying to take a bite from it.

"Nice clothes," Patches said with a giggle.

Elliot glanced down at his checkered pajamas. "I didn't have time to change into clothes before we were kidnapped."

"Pixie led."

"Huh?"

"You were Pixie led, not kidnapped exactly. Did you see a mist last night?"

"Yeah."

"That was the Pixies leading you to their snare."

Elliot folded his arms. "Tubs was Pixie led. I was Tubs led."

Patches frowned. "Humans know how to escape being Pixie led, right?"

Obviously, Elliot didn't know. "How?" he asked.

"Just turn your clothes inside out. It confuses them."

"I wasn't going to turn my clothes inside out in front of a bunch of Pixie girls," Elliot said.

"Don't worry. Princess Fidget would've gotten you here one way or another," Patches said, as if that should have made him feel better. "She always gets what she wants. What we must do now is figure out how to fix this."

"Do you think I should release Grissel?" Elliot asked.

"No!" Patches said. "Before long, he'd get the Goblins to start eating us again."

Which, Elliot agreed, would be bad. No matter what, releasing Grissel was not an option. "Any advice?" he asked.

Patches shrugged. "I don't know about them, but in school my teacher told us that hundreds of years ago, if two Pixies couldn't settle an argument, they took a 'time-out.' The winner won the argument, and it was done."

"Time-out," Elliot mumbled. "I know about those. So I guess to win, I just have to stay in time-out the longest?"

At just that moment, Mr. Willimaker appeared. His bushy gray eyebrows were pressed close together, telling Elliot he had not made any progress with Grissel. Princess Fidget poofed in immediately after. On either side of her were two larger Pixies with sour looks on their faces.

"Like, get rid of the Brownie king first," Fidget said to the Pixies with her. "Mind wipe the other boy if you can, and totally return him to the surface. If you can't, then get rid of him too."

The Pixies pulled out their wands and pointed them at Elliot, who backed up and stumbled over Tubs on the ground. He said, "Wait! Princess Fidget, I demand a time-out."

Her eyes narrowed. "A time-out?"

"Yeah. Me and Grissel together. If I win, you set me free. If he wins, I'll set him free."

"No, Your Highness," Mr. Willimaker cried, but it was too late.

Stretching her hand to study her nails, Fidget said, "Under the terms of a time-out, if you lose, Grissel goes free. And if he decides to leave you alive, which he probably won't, then you must remain here as my servant for, like, forever."

Elliot glared at Patches. She might have mentioned that. Still, it was better than being killed in here. "Okay," Elliot said. "I want a time-out."

Fidget clasped her tiny hands together. "What-ever. I'll prepare the battle zone. If you somehow survive the time-out with Grissel, which you probably won't, I'll totally have you for a servant, human."

"It looks like the rules are in Grissel's favor," Elliot said.

"Nobody ever said time-outs were fair," Fidget said, and then with a mischievous shrug added, "especially when I get to make the rules!"

When she poofed away, Elliot rushed to the bars. "Mr. Willimaker, what happens in a time-out?"

"It's a fight. When the time runs out, someone's usually dead. Isn't that what time-out means in your language?"

"No," Elliot said, slumping to the ground. "No, it isn't."

Chapter 9

Where Elliot Gets a Song Stuck in His Head

Elliot's twin brothers had spent most of their first six years of life either in time-out or doing something that deserved a time-out. Elliot had done his share of time-outs too. Something told him, however, that this time-out would be very different from sitting alone on a stool in the corner.

For one thing, no one had ever tried to kill him in time-out before, and Elliot's parents were very strict about not letting Elliot kill anyone, whether in time-out or not.

For another thing, time-outs were usually done alone, and Elliot was pretty sure every Pixie, Brownie, and Goblin in the Underworld had gathered around the Battle Zone to watch.

The Battle Zone was about as big as Elliot's schoolroom, but it was round and fenced in with thorny tree branches and had a dirt floor. Elliot had removed Reed's slippers for the fight. He'd never seen anyone win a battle to the death while wearing house slippers. He'd never seen anyone win a battle in red-checkered pajamas either, but he couldn't do anything about that.

Directly across from Elliot, Grissel paced in preparation for the fight. He hadn't changed much since Elliot had last seen him. A little rounder around the middle, maybe, due to his eating a lot of chocolate cake lately. But still the same shade of green skin, same bony face, same hatred of humans reflected in his eyes. He'd barely looked at Elliot since he was poofed here, but he was already drooling, hungry for revenge. The Goblins cheered loudly for him. The Brownies sat behind Elliot, cheering for him. The Pixies seemed to be cheering for a long battle, no matter who won. Then from somewhere nearby, Elliot heard, "You can take this one, Penster. Win it for the humans!"

Elliot turned. Even Tubs was cheering for him. Then Tubs yelled, "Besides, if you die, how will I get home?"

That was less helpful. Although just before Elliot was poofed to the Battle Zone, Tubs had given him some good advice: "If you can't beat him, just move around a lot until he gets tired of chasing you. I always hated it when you did that to me."

"Grissel doesn't need to chase me. Goblins scare you to death."

"But that only works if you're scared, right? Just think funny things and you'll be fine."

"Wow, Tubs," Elliot had said. "That's actually a good idea."

Tubs had stuck out his chest. "I'm smarter than all the kids in the whole first grade."

"But you're a seventh-grader."

"Duh." Tubs snorted. "I didn't say I was in their grade, I just said I'm smarter than them. And it *is* a good idea, so use it or else!"

Now Elliot waved at Tubs, who shook a fist back at him. Threatening to beat Elliot up if he didn't win was Tubs's style of cheering him on.

Fidget fluttered in from above them and landed in the center of the Battle Zone. For the time-out, she had chosen a bright yellow shirt with a hot pink skirt. She looked like she was dressed for a disco party. "Like, welcome to all Pixies, Goblins, and everyone else," she began, clearly forgetting that other than Tubs, "everyone else" was the Brownies. "We are so blown away by having a time-out today, which has totally not happened for over a hundred years."

A cheer rose from the Pixies. Not sure whether they should be celebrating this or not, the Goblins clapped a little, then lowered their hands when Grissel turned to glare at them. The Brownies remained silent.

Fidget continued, "So here are the rules. The time-out will last for ten minutes, because the awesomest stylist ever is coming to do my hair. If Grissel kills Elliot faster than that, it would be so radical, because then I'll have time to get my nails done too. If Elliot's still alive after the ten-minute time-out, he'll totally be my servant. Either way, Grissel goes free, and then he keeps his promise to me, and we'll, like, totally blow the Fairies to dust!" She forgot to mention what happened if Elliot survived. Maybe she didn't think there was any chance he would.

Both the Pixies and Goblins cheered loudly. The Brownies squirmed in their seats. Even they didn't expect Elliot to win.

"Happy thoughts, happy thoughts," Elliot mumbled. But his brain was in a fuzz. For some reason, all he could remember was the awful theme song to Fidget's favorite show, *Surfer Teen*.

> *Surfer Teen,*
> *Awesomest kid on the scene.*
> *Rockin' muscles lean and mean.*
> *You're Surfer Teen.*

"Like, when I say 'Time in,' then the battle begins," Fidget said.

"Happy thoughts," Elliot mumbled to the tune from *Surfer Teen*.

"Time in!" Fidget sliced her wand through the air, and sparks shot out from the end of it. The crowd cheered as she flew away and the battle began.

Grissel ran toward Elliot, but stopped in the center of the ring where Fidget had stood. With a low growl, he crouched on all fours. Elliot knew what was happening. He was preparing to scare Elliot to death.

Rockin' muscles lean and mean.

Grissel's bony skin began to bubble in rhythm.

Oddly, he bubbled to the rhythm of the lyrics stuck in Elliot's head.

Elliot started singing them: *"You're Surfer Teen..."*

As he sang, Elliot pictured Grissel as a surfer teen. Grissel on all fours on a surfboard. But Goblins hate water, so he'd have to balance on the surfboard so that no water splashed on him.

Maybe just because he was so tired, that the pictures he imagined seemed really funny. Funnier than Grissel was scary, and Elliot was laughing hard before he even finished the lyrics.

Grissel growled at Elliot, arching his back even higher. It should have been scary, but for some reason it wasn't. Maybe Elliot was laughing too hard to be scared. Now he was picturing Grissel wearing a swimsuit with tropical flowers. And sunglasses—he'd have to wear sunglasses! Pink ones that matched his swimsuit. If a green-skinned Goblin gets a suntan, does he turn olive green? What color is a sunburn? Mud color?

Tears came to Elliot's eyes as he laughed. His stomach ached from laughter.

"Nobody laughs at me," Grissel said, rising up to his full height. He lunged at Elliot with bare teeth. Elliot used the only weapon he had available to him. Spit. He spit on Grissel while Grissel was still in midair. The spit landed in Grissel's eye, and he fell to the ground, screaming and writhing in pain.

"Oh, that's so totally time out," Fidget said, fluttering into the ring from above. She stared down at Grissel, who was still helpless on the ground. "This is, like, such a bummer."

Elliot jumped into the air in celebration. So Grissel had not killed him, and the time-out was over. "That's it?" he said. "Then I won."

"Wrong," Grissel said. "I scared you to death. You're just slow at dying."

Elliot folded his arms. "Am not. I'll bet I could die really fast if you were any good at scaring me."

"I've been scary longer than you've been alive," Grissel said. "Just admit you've lost and die already, then I'll go free."

"Like, that's totally enough." Fidget flicked her wand at the crowd. "All of you just go away."

And with that, the entire audience disappeared. Elliot wasn't sure where they'd all gone. Somewhere safe, he hoped.

Grissel smiled wickedly at Elliot. "Now it's just you and me, little king."

But Fidget flew between them. "You had your chance, Goblin. You're so yesterday, and I'm already on tomorrow. Back you go to the Brownie jail."

Grissel's protest was only half spoken when Fidget poofed him away with her wand.

Elliot held up his hands, the way bad guys do when the cops say to freeze. Fidget sighed. "Don't be so lame, human. If I wanted to kill you, I'd have just done it already."

"You're letting me go home?"

"Hello?" Fidget rapped Elliot's head with her wand, then she pointed it at the Glimmering Forest. "Does it look like we've beaten the Fairies? You're not going home yet."

"I know you've got a Fairy problem," Elliot said, "but I've got a problem too, one named Cami Wortson. If you think Goblins are scary, you should see this girl when she gets a bad grade."

"Can Cami Wortson turn you inside out with a wave of her wand?"

Elliot clutched his stomach. Maybe if she had a wand she could. She'd probably enjoy doing it too.

Fidget folded her arms. "Let's get this straight, human. Even if this Cami Wortson has snakes for hair and spikes for teeth, I'm still the scariest girl you know. And if you want to go home, then you'll have to solve my problem first."

"You think I can get the Fairies out of Glimmering Forest? I can't even get my sister out of the bathroom in the morning."

"I'll take care of the Fairies. All I need from you is one little hair."

"My hair?" Elliot would shave himself bald if that's all it took to go home. It'd be hard to explain the baldness to his family, but it would be worth it.

Fidget sighed in a way that reminded Elliot of how stupid his question was. "Eww, gag me! I so totally don't want human hair. To keep the Fairies out of Glimmering Forest, all I need is one hair from their worst enemy—the Demon Kovol."

Chapter 10

Where Elliot Gets a Neck Ache

Dear Reader, if you've recently traveled to Greenland, you probably noticed the musk ox grazing nearby. The musk ox has two layers of hair, so even when it loses the outside layer, it still has plenty of hair left. The hair can be two to three feet long and sometimes drags on the ground. So if Fidget had ordered Elliot to steal a hair from a musk ox, as long as Elliot was nice about it, the musk ox probably wouldn't have cared.

But that's not what Fidget ordered.

She wanted a hair from a very different creature.

Elliot had about a hundred reasons why he wasn't going to snatch a hair from the Demon Kovol. For one thing, Kovol was supposed to be asleep for another thousand years. If he woke up to someone pulling his hair out, that was sure to start his day off badly, not to mention that he would definitely end Elliot's day in a very unpleasant way. And for another reason, everyone Elliot had ever asked about Kovol sounded like they'd rather face a dentist's drill without being numb than face ten seconds with Kovol.

Agatha the Hag had told Elliot that Kovol was the last of the Underworld Demons. He didn't know why Kovol was the last, and he didn't know why Kovol was sleeping. But Agatha had seemed certain that asleep was the way everyone in the Underworld wanted Kovol to remain.

Elliot didn't have time to tell Fidget why he wasn't going to snatch a hair from Kovol. She apparently had bigger problems to deal with. Fidget stamped her foot and whined, "Oh, fruit rot. I'm late for my hair stylist. Now it'll be wash and go. Not awesome!"

Elliot tried to say something before she fluttered away, but she cut him off and said, "Oh, and that other human with you— Tubs—he's staying here until you bring me the hair. Better hurry before I get bored and put him in time-out with a Troll." With that, she poofed Elliot away. He decided that he didn't like being poofed places. It made his stomach feel upside down. For all he knew, maybe it was.

But the question for now was where Fidget had sent him. He was standing on some grass near a small town set on a hill, where it looked as if little homes had been made from caves in the hillside. A maze of dirt paths went from one house to another, so it would be nearly impossible to travel anywhere without stopping at a dozen homes along the way. Wherever he was, Elliot decided he liked this place. He wouldn't fit inside any of the homes, but it was a friendly looking town. All it needed was a good ice cream store and it would have been perfect.

"Elliot?" Patches came running up from behind him. "I mean, Your Highness. You're free?"

"Is this Burrowsville?" Despite the serious task that lay ahead of him, Elliot couldn't help but feel excited about seeing the land where he was king.

"This is Burrowsville. Your home away from home, I hope. You can come to our cave for dinner. My mother really wants to meet you. She just made a fresh batch of turnip juice this morning. Squished it with her own toes."

"Yum." Elliot smiled grimly. "Maybe another time. I need to—"

"Your Highness?" Fudd came running over a hill and bowed low before Elliot. Back when Fudd was a bad Brownie trying to get Elliot killed, it made sense that he should also be mean-looking. His long, crooked nose and thin slits for eyes seemed a little unusual for a good Brownie, who was most definitely not trying to kill Elliot. But nothing could be done about Fudd's face, so Elliot had gotten used to it. Fudd clasped his hands together and added, "How did—oh, Princess Fidget must have sent you here."

"I need to meet with you and Mr. Willimaker," Elliot said. "Privately."

Fudd nodded, and then said to Patches, "Take the king to Burrow Cave. He should fit comfortably in there."

Ten minutes later, Elliot disagreed with Fudd. He did *not* fit comfortably inside the cave. It was easily wide enough, but he had to tilt his head in order to sit up. He could lie down for the meeting, but that didn't seem very king-like. Mr. Willimaker and Fudd had offered to bring in some Brownies to dig the floor lower for him, but there was no time.

With his head tilted almost down to his shoulder, Elliot explained what Fidget wanted him to do.

"Get a hair from Kovol?" Mr. Willimaker exclaimed. "You can't."

"I have to," Elliot said. "She still has Tubs in the jail."

Mr. Willimaker shook his head. "No, I really meant that you can't. Humans aren't allowed in Demon Territory. We don't get many human visitors, of course, but it's still the rule. There's even Elfish guards and a big sign telling humans to stay out."

Fudd clamped a hand on Mr. Willimaker's shoulder and said, "A Brownie could do it." Mr. Willimaker frowned at Fudd. He didn't look convinced.

"How dangerous is Demon Territory if the Demon is asleep?" Elliot asked.

"How dangerous is a lion's den if the lion's asleep?" Mr. Willimaker responded. "And if the lion's really hungry because he hasn't eaten for a thousand years? And then you go up and ask him for just one little hair? You think he'll just smile and hand it over?"

"Then I'm not sending you there for a job I have to do," Elliot said. "If you'll come with me as far as the border of Demon Territory, I'll do the rest."

"Your Highness," Mr. Willimaker said, "it's not worth it, not for Tubs Lawless."

"Tubs is only here because of me," Elliot said, sitting up straight and banging his ear on the roof of the cave. He tilted his head a bit more and then said, "I have to do this."

"Then we'll leave first thing in the morning," Fudd said. "First, Your Highness, I believe you need a good sleep, and you look hungry. Your subjects, the Brownies, would like to honor you with a royal feast tonight."

The closest thing to a royal feast Elliot had ever had was when the power went out before Wendy had finished burning dinner and the food came out about right. And he was hungry now.

Fudd stood. "I'll take care of dinner plans." With that, he poofed away.

Mr. Willimaker stood as well. "And please don't be offended, Your Highness, but checkered pajamas aren't the best way to meet your subjects. May I suggest we have a tailor prepare some clothes for you?"

Elliot looked down at his pajamas. "Yes, please."

Mr. Willimaker bowed to Elliot, then said, "Sir, don't worry about Kovol's hair. With Fudd and me by your side, nothing can go wrong."

He poofed away, leaving Elliot alone in the cave. Somehow, Mr. Willimaker's words didn't make Elliot feel better. If he'd learned anything since becoming king of the Brownies, it was that something could always go wrong.

Chapter 11

Where Elliot Gets an Itch and a Flashlight

Your tailors haven't sewn for kids lately," Elliot said to Mr. Willimaker as he faced a mirror. It was the largest mirror in Burrowsville, but Elliot could still see only part of himself in it at a time. And he'd had to dress behind some bushes. He wasn't positive someone saw him, but he had definitely heard giggling nearby.

Mr. Willimaker agreed. "It seems human fashion has changed over the last century or two."

For pants, Elliot wore breeches that gathered at his calf. He had a pullover shirt with full sleeves that gathered at his wrists and a vest that buttoned up the front. "I look like a pirate," he said.

"Don't be silly," Mr. Willimaker said. "Pirates never wore vests like that. You look like a pioneer."

The only things Elliot didn't hate were his shoes. They fit him perfectly and were very comfortable. Elliot tugged at his shirt. Maybe if he didn't tuck it in, it wouldn't look so much like something his great-great-great-great-grandpa would've worn while picking up cow pies on the plains.

"I'm sorry, Your Highness," Mr. Willimaker said. "We'll find some patterns for modern-day boys so that next time you're kidnapped—"

"Next time?" Elliot asked. "Thanks for the clothes, but next time I'd like to come to the Underworld on my own."

Fudd entered the room. "King Elliot? Dinner is ready. We're eating outside, where you'll be most comfortable."

Elliot nodded. If he was half starved before, then he was all the way starved by now. He forgot all about his clothes and followed Fudd outside. He expected most of the Brownies to be at the royal feast, but he had no idea how many Brownies there were. When he had used the Brownies to help end the Goblin war, the stronger ones had come, but the rest had stayed back.

"Is this all of them?" Elliot whispered to Mr. Willimaker.

"We know you'd rather be home," Mr. Willimaker said, "but for us Brownies, the king has come and today is a holiday. Everyone wants to see you."

A cheer rose through the crowd when they saw Elliot enter. Long rows of tables lined a large grassy field. Hundreds of Brownies of every size and age stood near the tables.

Babies sat on their fathers' shoulders. Younger Brownie children stood on chairs to get a better look at their king. The only thing the Brownies all had in common was their various shades of gray hair, sticking up in wild directions. Together, they looked like a field of unmowed gray grass. Elliot had never guessed there would be so many of them.

At the head of the crowd, a table had been specially built for Elliot. Fudd pulled at Elliot's bulky sleeve and said, "We tried to have a throne made for you, but there just wasn't time. We did find a giant toadstool that was about your size."

The royal toadstool was in front of Elliot's seat at the table. A red satin cloth lay over the top for him to sit on, and blue flower petals surrounded the base of it. "Looks comfortable," Elliot said, grinning. "This is a great throne."

He went to sit, but Mr. Willimaker touched his arm. "Aren't you going to say anything to the Brownies?"

"Huh? Oh, sure." Elliot faced the Brownies, who all fell to their knees when they saw he was about to speak. "You don't have to do that," he said. Slowly they rose again, and he continued, "Um, so thanks for letting me be your king. I'll try to do a good job."

The Brownies cheered again and a cry rose up of "Long live King Elliot!"

"That was quite a speech," Mr. Willimaker said. "Very inspirational and, uh, easy to remember."

"Now it's time to eat," Fudd said. "I hope you're hungry."

Elliot was so hungry that he was almost ready to eat his shirt (which might be one good way to get rid of it). Back at home, if there was ever any decent food, you had to grab it fast before someone else got it. But here, Elliot noticed, the Brownies were waiting for him to eat first. The only time Elliot's family had waited for him to eat first was last April Fool's Day, when the twins had switched the sugar and salt. Elliot was three bites into his cold cereal before he realized that wasn't sugar on his flakes.

When Elliot was seated on his royal toadstool, then the Brownies sat. Immediately a Brownie woman put a plate of food in front of him. It was full of bread, a yellowish fruit, and a lot of green vegetables Elliot didn't recognize. All the Brownies were watching him, including the woman who had just served him.

"Yum." Elliot picked up his fork and took a bite of the green vegetables. They tasted like Kyle and Cole's mud pies, only with the unexpected aftertaste of peppermint. "Mmmmm," he said, doing his best to convince the woman that he liked the strange food. "Really good."

There probably weren't any Quack Shacks in the Underworld. Too bad. French fries sounded great right now.

"Have you tried the turnip juice yet?" Mr. Willimaker asked.

It looked like apple juice, but it was more syrupy, and Elliot thought he saw a turnip root floating on top of his juice. But he put on a smile, lifted his cup, and said, "Cheers!"

Mr. Willimaker toasted Elliot in return, and they both drank. Elliot's plan was to finish the whole thing in one awful gulp, but he was surprised at his first taste that it wasn't bad. Not that he'd want to replace chocolate milk with turnip juice or anything, but he wouldn't mind it so much if they gave him some more.

"That turnip juice is sort of like me," said a woman walking up to him. "We're both better than we first appear."

Elliot looked up. "Agatha!"

The first time Elliot had met Agatha, she was a has-been Hag who couldn't quite get her curses to work. She was also the closest thing to what Elliot imagined a real witch might look like. After a few days, Agatha had remembered how to curse again, and eventually Elliot saw what a truly beautiful woman she was.

Beside Elliot, Mr. Willimaker stood and greeted her with a polite bow. "Agatha, we weren't expecting you."

"The king of the Brownies finally comes to the Underworld. I wouldn't miss this moment," she said, then pointed a crooked finger at Mr. Willimaker. "But for forgetting to invite me, this curse I leave with you today: I am a Hag and here's what I think. You'll find some trouble when you take a drink."

Mr. Willimaker looked at his cup of turnip juice, frowned, and then pushed it aside, just to be safe.

Fudd jumped up and pulled out his chair on the other side of Elliot. "Take my chair, please, my lady."

"I can't stay," Agatha said. "I just need to speak to Elliot for a moment."

Elliot stood. All the Brownies were still watching him, and he had a sudden itch on his backside. He wondered what kings were supposed to do when they needed to scratch in an embarrassing place and everyone was watching them.

"Pay attention, Elliot," Agatha said.

Elliot turned to her, hoping that whatever she had to say was so important it would help him forget the itch.

"I have a gift for you," she said, rummaging through a bag hanging from her arm.

A gift? Maybe it was a bottom scratcher.

"I heard a rumor that you have agreed to help the Pixies," she continued. "I have a guess at what they've asked you to do, but I'm not going to say what I think it is because I can't do anything more to help you. Do you understand?"

"Sure," Elliot said, although he really didn't understand at all.

"Ahh, here it is." She pulled a flashlight from her bag.

"Oh," he said, reaching for it. "Thanks."

Agatha yanked the flashlight away from him and added, "This isn't a human flashlight. It's not for seeing *in* the dark. It will see *through* the dark."

81

Same thing, Elliot thought, but he said nothing.

Agatha continued. "It can be turned on only once, so you don't want to use it until you're sure you need it."

Fudd tapped Elliot's arm. "Like when it's light outside. Whatever you do, don't turn it on in the light."

"Right." Elliot figured that was obvious.

"If it's a little light and a little dark, don't turn it on then either," Fudd added. "Or if it's mostly dark but you can still see."

"Got it," Elliot said.

Agatha continued, "This flashlight doesn't run on batteries. It runs on the sun."

"There's no sun in the Underworld," Elliot said.

"But the flashlight doesn't know that," Agatha said with a sigh. "Honestly, Elliot, I thought you were a smart boy. The flashlight doesn't know why it works, it just does. Why would you think the flashlight knows anything at all?"

Elliot shrugged, still confused.

"Once you turn the flashlight on, it gets its power from the sun at the surface of the earth. It will remain on until the sun is blocked by a solar eclipse. Then the light goes out and the flashlight is used up."

With that, Agatha handed Elliot the flashlight. It was heavier than it looked and made of a shiny silver metal that was a bit greasy.

"The grease isn't from the metal," Agatha explained. "I had fried chicken before coming here and forgot to wash my fingers. Sorry about that."

"Oh, no problem," Elliot said, wiping the flashlight with his shirt. He really didn't care if he ruined the shirt. "Thanks for this."

"I owed you one. You helped me when I was in your world. I'll help you now that you're in mine. Now, sit back down and finish your dinner. You have a long trip ahead of you tomorrow."

Agatha disappeared in a puff of smoke (sometimes called "poofed in a puff," but Elliot doesn't like to think of it that way, because it sounds like something one might do in a toilet). He smiled. The itch was gone. Maybe good luck was finally turning his way.

Chapter 12

Where Fudd Stays Home

Elliot slept in Burrow Cave that night. Mr. Willimaker apologized that his own home wasn't large enough for Elliot, but added that it was probably a good thing, since Patches would only keep him up all night with questions.

Elliot was glad for the chance to be alone. He'd been awake most of the previous night, either from Tubs's snoring or with the whole kidnapped-to-the-Underworld thing. And tonight the Brownies had kept him awake very late trying to feed him, or wanting to ask him questions about life on the surface, or thanking him for ending the Goblin war.

Elliot was glad for the time alone, because he really wanted to think about how he was going to sneak into Demon Territory and pluck a hair off the head of the most dangerous Demon of all time.

He wanted to think about it, but he was too tired. He soon fell asleep between thoughts of Kovol and whether Harold the Shapeshifter had been able to fool his family that day pretending to be Elliot. Harold might be able to fool his sister and brothers, and maybe even his dad. But not his mom. One time, Elliot hadn't wanted to worry her about the black eye he got when Tubs pushed him into a door. So Elliot wore sunglasses to dinner. Didn't fool his mom one bit. Could Harold fool her?

The next morning, Fudd and Mr. Willimaker met Elliot at the mouth of Burrow Cave. Mr. Willimaker was kneeling in front of a large sack, making sure he had packed everything he thought they should bring on their journey.

"Squash greens, turnip juice, branberries—" Mr. Willimaker looked up at Elliot. "Is there anything else you'd like me to bring, Your Highness?"

"Is there any bread left over from last night?" Elliot asked. The bread had been good.

"I'll check." Mr. Willimaker bowed slightly at Elliot and then poofed away.

Fudd tapped Elliot on the shoulder, then handed Elliot a cup with a cream-colored, foamy drink inside. It looked like a vanilla shake. "Breakfast, Your Highness."

Elliot took a small first swallow—just in case it tasted like squash greens or turnip juice, which he hadn't quite decided to like. But this was delicious. A perfect drink, really. It was different from a vanilla shake, maybe even better. He drank the rest in only a few swallows.

"That was great," he told Fudd. "What do you call it?"

"Mushroom Surprise," Fudd said.

Elliot coughed. He was surprised, all right.

"This is a favorite breakfast for Brownies," Fudd added. "I always feel it's wise to drink your daily dose of mushrooms."

"Sure," Elliot agreed. "Why not?"

"Just so you know, this wasn't made with poisonous mushrooms," Fudd said, holding up his own cup. "I made the same drink for myself."

"I know. I trust you." Elliot handed his cup back to Fudd, who held on to it with Elliot for a moment and whispered, "Thank you, sir," before poofing the cups away.

Next, Fudd folded his short, chubby arms, then unfolded

them, and finally sort of held them halfway folded. "King Elliot, please don't go."

"Don't worry," Elliot said. "I'll come back. Kovol won't wake up." Elliot hoped if he said the words enough, they would come true.

"But what if the Fairies find out you're helping the Pixies? They won't like it."

"Even if they did find out, what could the Fairies do to me that the Pixies haven't already done?"

Fudd shook his head. "King Elliot, I have to tell you something." Then he fell silent.

"What?" Elliot finally asked.

Fudd coughed. "I own this book, *The Guidebook to Evil Plans*. It clearly states, 'Choose your friendships carefully. Good friends might weaken your evil plans. On the other hand, evil friends might destroy you so that they can take over your plans (page 16).'"

Elliot waited for Fudd to explain why he was saying this. Finally, Fudd shrugged and said, "There's nothing else. I was just quoting."

Elliot asked, "Fudd, do you support me as king?"

Fudd's beady eyes shifted. "I wish you didn't have to ask, Your Highness. My point is that you need to be careful out there. The Fairies want Glimmering Woods just as much as the Pixies do. They won't be happy about this."

"They can join the club," Elliot said. "*I'm* not happy about this either." Then he jumped a bit as Mr. Willimaker poofed back on his right side and Patches appeared on his left.

"I found bread," Mr. Willimaker said.

"No, *I* found it," Patches corrected him. She held a large bundle in her arms. "Actually, I put together a whole bunch of human food. Sorry for my dad, Elliot. He doesn't know all the food humans like."

"I just drank Mushroom Surprise," Elliot said. "I liked that."

Patches made a face. "Don't you know what the surprise is?"

"No."

She grinned. "You will."

Elliot took the bundle from Patches. Whatever she'd put in there, it smelled good. And Elliot had the flashlight from Agatha tucked in his belt. Maybe this trip wouldn't be such a big deal after all.

"Are we ready then?" Fudd asked. "Ready to go to our deaths, no doubt, but we'll see some nice sights along the way."

"Only Mr. Willimaker and I are going," Elliot said.

"But Your Highness," Fudd protested. "I owe this to you."

"You can owe it to me later. I need Mr. Willimaker to show me the way, but if I don't come back, then someone will need to stay here as king."

Fudd shook his head. "I don't want to become king that way. Not anymore."

Elliot smiled and tapped Agatha's flashlight. "Don't worry. I have the flashlight, and Kovol is asleep. I'm sure it won't be as hard as everyone thinks."

"Let me come with you," Patches said.

"No," Mr. Willimaker and Elliot said together. Mr. Willimaker added, "Besides, you have school tomorrow, and no Shapeshifter is available to take your place."

Elliot and Patches both groaned, although for very different reasons. Then Patches slumped to the ground and folded her arms. "Fine, but I could've helped."

To his right, Elliot noticed a winding road paved in yellow bricks. "Oh. A yellow brick road. I suppose we should follow it out of Burrowsville, right?"

Mr. Willimaker grabbed his arm to hold him back. "Are you crazy? Don't you know where that leads?"

Elliot shook his head. "No. Where?"

Mr. Willimaker shuddered. "No Brownie who's walked that path has ever returned. We call it the Yellow Brick Road of Doom." He pointed to a hill leading in the opposite direction. "We go that way, Your Highness."

"Then let's go." Elliot took his first steps, and Mr. Willimaker quickly caught up to walk beside him. "How long will it take for us to get there?"

Mr. Willimaker pulled a map out of his pocket. "If we don't stop to see any sights along the way and we keep up a good pace, maybe a week."

"A week?" Elliot asked. "That long?"

"I said *maybe,*" Mr. Willimaker said. "I could be wrong. It might take us much, much longer than that."

Chapter 13

Where Elliot Thinks about the Number Fifty

B efore Elliot had become king of the Brownies, he'd done a lot of running. Mostly running away from Tubs, who would have left bruises on any part of Elliot's body he could catch. Reasons like that help a kid run away fast.

But Tubs hadn't chased Elliot since the end of the Goblin war, and Elliot was a little out of shape. Now he was thinking that Burrowsville had a lot of hills. Going down them wasn't bad, except the next hill up always seemed to be a little taller than the one before it. At least the bright colors of the Underworld trees and flowers kept things interesting. Obviously there was no sun above them, but everything was warm and light, and the sky had a cool, pastel yellow glow.

It took them a while to get out of Burrowsville. As they walked the winding road through the town, Brownies came out to greet Elliot and to thank him for what he'd done in ending the Goblin war. Mr. Willimaker pointed out that many of the younger Brownies had never seen a human up close before. After a few hours they left the border of Burrowsville and entered what Mr. Willimaker called the "Underworlderness."

There weren't a lot of trees here, but the narrow trail was lined with blueberry bushes even taller than Elliot. For nearly a mile, the thick bushes marked the trail. Elliot and Mr. Willimaker ate a lunch of them as they walked.

Mr. Willimaker tried to talk with Elliot that afternoon, but Elliot was deep in thought. It was cool to have seen Burrowsville, and Elliot was proud of the fact that he'd beaten Grissel in the time-out—not that he could tell any of his family that—but he still wished he were home. He wondered whether the twins had dug any more mud pits, or whether his Uncle Rufus had returned to his habit of stealing shiny things, or what Wendy had burned for dinner last night. Funny that he missed her burned food. Maybe she'd messed up his taste buds, and burned food was starting to taste normal to him.

And something in his stomach had been rumbling for a while, as though his own personal volcano were trapped inside. He took two more steps, and then the volcano erupted in the form of a gigantic burp. Mr. Willimaker ducked, and the burped-out air hit a large blueberry bush that promptly wilted and died.

"Did I do that?" Elliot asked.

"More correctly, your Mushroom Surprise drink did that. Better a bush than me, I always say." Mr. Willimaker brushed off his clothes and continued walking. "Warn me the next time you feel that coming, please."

"Sorry," Elliot said, although he secretly thought his toxic burp was pretty cool.

"Your Highness, if I may—" Mr. Willimaker began.

"We've got a long walk ahead of us," Elliot said. "You don't have to call me that. Just use my name."

"Yes, Your Highness. Anyway, if I may ask, I'm a little unclear about your plan to get the hair from Kovol's head."

"I don't have a plan," Elliot said. "I think I'll just have to figure it out when we get there."

"Understood. But if you did have a plan, what would it be?"

Elliot sighed. "The thing is, I've never been to Demon Territory. I've never seen Kovol before, and I really don't know anything about him other than that he's supposed to be asleep. And to be honest, I've never tried to pull a hair out of anyone's head before, especially while they're asleep."

"Ah," Mr. Willimaker said. "To be honest, I haven't done that before either. Not the sort of thing a polite creature does, is it?"

Elliot smiled. "No." Tubs had pulled a chunk of his hair out once, in kindergarten. Actually, Tubs had put a whole

glob of superglue on his own hand. When Elliot teased him about it, Tubs smacked Elliot in the head, and his hand stuck to Elliot's hair. Then when he tore his hand away, a lot of Elliot's hair had come with it. Later that day, Elliot's mom had shaved the rest of his hair really short to cover up how many bald patches there were.

They continued to walk, with Mr. Willimaker pointing out some of the sights in the Underworld. "If we went south tomorrow, we'd come to a lake where the Mermaids like to swim. You can't fish there, though. Turns out the Mermaids don't like to be fished." A couple of hours later, Mr. Willimaker pointed in another direction. "See those mountains in the distance? The Dwarves live there."

"Are there any Mermaids or Dwarves on the surface world?" Elliot asked.

"A Mermaid finds her way to the surface every now and then, but not in the numbers there used to be. You'll find Dwarves anywhere there's enough treasure to be found, though the Underworld is still rich in valuable stones. If humans knew how many diamonds were down here, they'd have found a way into our land ages ago."

"I have a question," Elliot said. "How is there light so far under the earth, and air I can breathe? This is a lot like the surface world, but with no humans."

"It's the combined magic of all Underworld creatures,"

Mr. Willimaker said. "Everyone gives a little, and together we have a much nicer life than most humans would expect. If they knew we had a life down here, of course."

"Does it bother you about humans?" Elliot asked. "I mean, that most humans don't believe you exist?"

"It's a good thing, actually," Mr. Willimaker said. "Hundreds of years ago when humans did believe in us, life was far more difficult. Now our only problem is the way your books and movies talk about us. You'd be surprised how wrong you are most of the time. To be fair, I suppose our books and movies get a few things wrong about humans too. For example, I don't suppose humans can leap over tall buildings in a single jump?"

Elliot smiled. "Maybe super humans. But I don't think they're real."

Mr. Willimaker shrugged. "Not long ago, you didn't think Brownies were real either." He checked his map. "What say we stop here for supper?"

"Sure." Elliot dropped his bag to the ground and untied the knot holding it together. Inside were apples, blueberries, cucumbers, and carrots. Naturally, Patches had also snuck in a large bag of pickles. Elliot pulled one out and began munching on it. "Mr. Willimaker," he asked, "what do you know about Shadow Men?"

Mr. Willimaker, who was eating something that looked

like an orange artichoke, stopped chewing. He swallowed hard, then in a low voice said, "They're Kovol's army. They guard him in his sleep, which means they haven't left Demon Territory in over a thousand years. Few creatures live through an encounter with the Shadow Men, so most of what we know is from the old writings. My own great-grandfather was killed trying to fight them."

"Sorry," Elliot mumbled.

"It happened a thousand years ago, so it's an old memory now. There was a great war in which all Underworld creatures united against the Demons. They would've lost too, if not for an agreement Kovol made that put him to sleep."

"What agreement?" Elliot asked.

"A human sorcerer named Minthred got involved in the war. I don't know the terms of the agreement, I'm afraid, just that Kovol went to sleep, and the Shadow Men have watched over him ever since." Mr. Willimaker paused to finish his artichoke. Then he added, "How will we get past the Shadow Men, Your Highness?"

Elliot shrugged. "We'll go in the daytime. I figure Shadow Men are probably night creatures, since in the daytime there aren't as many shadows where they can hide."

"How do you know about Shadow Men?"

"Harold the Shapeshifter turned into one when I was still on the surface. He was scary, but I beat Grissel trying to scare me to death. I can beat the Shadow Men too, if I have to."

"Even in the form of a Shadow Man, he was still just a Shapeshifter," Mr. Willimaker warned. "And there was only one of him. Kovol's army is probably much larger."

"How much larger?"

Mr. Willimaker held out his hands. "I don't know. It's been a thousand years since anybody's seen one. I'm sure their numbers are smaller than before, but you could face an army of fifty or more."

Fifty was a lot. Elliot sighed and tried not to think about that. Because if he did, he would have to admit that he didn't know how an eleven-year-old kid and a Brownie had any chance against fifty of the scariest creatures he'd ever met.

Chapter 14

Where Elliot Doesn't Get
His Drink of Water

Mr. Willimaker finished his supper at about the same time Elliot decided he might have lost his appetite for good.

"Didn't you like the food Patches packed for you?" Mr. Willimaker asked. "I tried to tell her."

"No, the food was good," Elliot said. "I'm just not hungry."

"You have Shadow Men on your mind?"

"A little." Elliot pressed his lips together. "All we have to do is sneak past them, get a hair from Kovol, and sneak out."

Mr. Willimaker smiled. "I wish it were going to be as easy as you make it sound. But if we do survive, it'll make a grand story for the Brownies." He stood and brushed off his clothes. "It's getting dark. Are you cold?"

Elliot wasn't. If anything, the clothes the Brownies had made for him locked heat in. "Did you want to make a fire?"

Mr. Willimaker shook his head. "It's usually warm in the Underworld, but a little light would be nice."

"I have the flashlight from Agatha," Elliot said. "Though with my luck, the next eclipse will happen five minutes after I turn it on, so let's wait until we really need it."

Mr. Willimaker snapped his fingers together. When he did, a spark of light remained on his thumb. He pressed his thumb to a stick, and it lit. Then Mr. Willimaker gathered a few other sticks together in a pile, and the light passed to them as well.

"Is that a magic fire?" Elliot asked.

"It's only light." Mr. Willimaker passed his hand through the center of the light. "There's no heat, and it won't burn anything. The light won't last long, but it'll do until we fall asleep."

"Can you make another fire?" Elliot wanted one to play with.

"Not for a few minutes. I need to recharge."

Elliot ran his hand through the center of the light as well. It was no warmer than the air, and yet it flickered on the sticks as a fire would. "Cool," he whispered. "I wish I had magic."

"All Underworld creatures have their own kinds of magic," Mr. Willimaker said. "Brownies aren't that powerful compared to Pixies or Fairies, or even Goblins. Elves have only a little magic but are more powerful in other ways. Same with the Dwarves. A Leprechaun has quite a bit of magic, and yet a human could easily overcome one if he knew how."

"How many Underworld creatures exist?" Elliot asked. "Are all the myths true?"

"There are creatures down here that humans know nothing about and some creatures that you know more about than you think." Mr. Willimaker shrugged. "I'm not sure how many of us there are. The Underworld is very big and not very well explored. Most of us keep to ourselves."

Elliot used his bundle as a pillow and laid back on it. Had he been sleeping on the surface, he would have expected to see stars, but the sky here was only black.

"I miss the moon," he said.

Mr. Willimaker lay on his own bundle near Elliot. "Wait for it to get a bit darker. The Star Dancers, creatures of the night, provide us with the night sky. I think you'll like it."

And he was right. After about a half hour, the Underworld became dark enough that Mr. Willimaker's cool fire was the only light around. Elliot stared at the sky again, but now it became painted in streaks of thin neon colors. Bright lines of blue, green, and orange raced across the sky, slowly fading as new colors were drawn over the top of them.

"Those are Star Dancers?" Elliot asked. "I don't think I've ever heard of them."

"They never go to the surface world," Mr. Willimaker said. "Why would they when they can have this much fun down here?"

"I like the Underworld," Elliot said. "If I survive Kovol, I might come back again one day. Fudd said the Brownies would build me a home here that's my size."

Mr. Willimaker was quiet for a moment, and then he said, "Your Highness, I want to talk to you about Fudd."

Elliot leaned up on his elbows. "What's the matter?"

"I hope it's nothing. Ever since the Goblin war ended, I believe Fudd has been sincere in trying to earn back your trust. But last night, after the royal feast, I overheard something that worries me. I believe the Fairies had a meeting with Fudd. He worked with them for years under Queen Bipsy, you know."

"I didn't know," Elliot said. That wasn't a question he had even thought about asking.

"Yes, well, the Fairies know you're down here. They asked Fudd why."

"What did he say?" Elliot asked.

"He said he couldn't tell them anything, but then they said they already knew the Pixies brought you here and they weren't happy about it. You see, the Fairies want the Glimmering Woods too. If they think you're helping the Pixies, they'll be upset."

"But I don't have a choice," Elliot said. "The Pixies have Tubs."

"I know, but the Fairies might not understand that," Mr. Willimaker said. "Fairies aren't the most forgiving creatures. They reminded Fudd about an old treaty the Brownies have with both the Pixies and Fairies, promising not to get involved in any fights between them. They told Fudd to stop you, or else they would."

Elliot groaned. "And what did Fudd say?"

Mr. Willimaker shrugged. "He told them he'd think about it. I don't know what he's decided."

"Doesn't sound good," Elliot said.

"No, it doesn't," Mr. Willimaker agreed.

They stared at the streaks for a while longer, although now that Elliot wondered whether Fudd had betrayed him again, the streaks didn't seem so bright and colorful. He sighed and said, "I don't think I'll get much sleep tonight."

"Cheer up, Your Highness," Mr. Willimaker said. "Other than the Brownies, I can think of at least five Underworld creatures who aren't trying to kill you right now."

"Great."

"Try to get some sleep," Mr. Willimaker mumbled. "I'll have breakfast ready when you wake up, and sn…"

Whatever "sn…" meant, Elliot wasn't going to find out. Mr. Willimaker was asleep before he finished the word.

Elliot slept better that night than he thought he would. He woke up to a cheery sunrise, or whatever it was in the Underworld that provided light. Morning magic, perhaps. He would have liked another cup of Fudd's Mushroom Surprise, although if Mr. Willimaker was right and Fudd couldn't be trusted, he probably shouldn't take anything else Fudd offered him.

Mr. Willimaker greeted Elliot when he sat up. "Awake, Your Highness? My apologies, I expected you to sleep awhile longer."

"Hard to sleep when you're hunting a Demon," Elliot said.

"Ah, yes." Mr. Willimaker said. "My cousin once said the same thing about hunting for delicious burbleberries. Although to be fair, burbleberries won't rip your arms off if you get close to them."

Elliot turned to Mr. Willimaker, who was finishing getting dressed. He looked as fresh and clean as ever. Elliot, on the other hand, thought he could smell his own body odor, and something sticky was on his cheek.

Mr. Willimaker hurried over to unwrap his bundle. "I saw a stream a little ways back. Maybe I can heat some water for a warm mint broth." As Mr. Willimaker pulled two cups from his bag, his ears suddenly perked up at the side of his head, the way a dog's might when it hears something.

"I don't mean to alarm you," Mr. Willimaker whispered, "but is there any chance that noise came from you?"

Elliot hadn't heard anything. "What noise?"

"That rustling noise. I was hoping that perhaps it was you over in those bushes."

"It's not me," Elliot said.

"Are you sure?" Mr. Willimaker's ears were at full attention now, then they relaxed and he added, "It was probably nothing. A rodent or a snake perhaps."

Elliot pulled his feet in close to him. He didn't like snakes. He didn't trust anything that could move on the ground without legs.

Mr. Willimaker tapped the cups. "I'll get some water. Won't be long." Then he walked away toward the stream.

Only a minute later, Elliot heard a "Hamph!" and a loud "No!" Then a small puff of smoke rose in the air and everything went silent. Elliot hoped it wasn't a snake that had gotten to Mr. Willimaker, because that would have to be some freaky large snake. He ran in the direction Mr. Willimaker had gone, calling his name, but there was no answer. Then he ran to the stream, but it didn't look as if Mr. Willimaker had gotten this far. At least, no footprints were in the mud other than Elliot's.

Elliot turned back the way he had come. Under a bush he saw the two cups Mr. Willimaker must have dropped.

"Mr. Willimaker?" Elliot called again. What had happened to him?

He picked up the cups and then saw a small note hanging from a branch of the bush. He plucked it off and read:

To the king of the Brownies—

By helping the Pixies, you are in violation of a treaty agreeing to stay out of any fighting over Glimmering Woods. Therefore, we have taken the Brownie, Mr. Willimaker, and will hold him as our captive until you also do something for the Fairies. We want a sock off the foot of the Demon Kovol. It shouldn't be a problem for you. We hear you're going to see him anyway.

Refuse to help us and you will never see Mr. Willimaker again. Should you fail with the Demon Kovol, no one will ever see you again.

Cheers!

The Fairies

Elliot crumpled the note into his pocket and yelled again, "Mr. Willimaker!" Then he yelled, "Fairies! I want to talk to you!"

But there was no answer.

He was alone in the Underworld, with no map either back to Burrowsville or ahead to Demon Territory. And he thought he heard a sound nearby. Something was coming toward him.

Where Elliot Is Clever Enough to Find Gripping Mud

Elliot hurried back to camp and gathered up both his and Mr. Willimaker's bundles. With his arms full, he began racing in the direction they'd been walking yesterday. He didn't know if he was still walking toward Demon Territory or not. But he did know he was moving away from whatever was following him.

Maybe it was Goblins, who knew he was alone and wanted revenge for his ending the Goblin war.

Maybe it was Fairies, coming to capture him before he could find Kovol.

Maybe it was the ice cream man on his secret Underworld route. That'd be cool, but he sort of doubted it. Elliot didn't have money for ice cream anyway.

Elliot ran so quickly through the bushes that he lost track of where he was going. All that mattered was getting away.

Then he burst into a small clearing and took a step onto something that wasn't hard ground.

It was a kind of mud, but no ordinary mud. His foot sank into the mud almost up to his knee. His second foot landed in the mud before he had time to stop, and he went in up to his thigh.

He didn't think he was in quicksand. Elliot had never been caught in quicksand before, due to the fact that there was no quicksand in Sprite's Hollow. But this wasn't sand at all. It was mud, and the mud seemed to be holding him in. The more he struggled, the more tightly the mud held on.

"King Elliot? It's me. Where are you?"

Elliot turned his head toward the sound. It wasn't Goblins or Fairies chasing him. It was Patches, who had disobeyed both him and her father to follow them into the Underworlderness. But she was about to save his life, so he decided to ignore her rule-breaking.

"I'm here," he called. "I need help!"

Patches poofed from wherever she was to stand on solid ground near Elliot. "Oh," she said. "Gripping mud."

"That's what this is?"

She giggled. "In case you didn't know, you're not supposed to walk on it."

"Now you tell me. How do I get out?"

Patches giggled again. "You can't. Well, I mean you can't get out by yourself. The more you try, the more you'll get stuck."

"So can you get me out?"

"If I get you out, then you can't get mad at me for following you, okay?"

Elliot smiled. "If you hadn't followed me, I'd be stuck here forever."

Patches knelt on the ground. "Okay, so here's how it works. I'm going to hand you a branch. You have to let me pull you out by myself. Don't help me at all. Anything you do will only make the mud hold you tighter."

"I'm pretty heavy for you," Elliot said.

"I'm pretty strong for me too." Patches snapped off a branch of a nearby tree and held it out to Elliot. "Just hold on."

Elliot held to the branch. Once Patches started to loosen him from the mud, he wiggled his legs to work his body upward. Instantly, the gripping mud pulled him down again.

"You might be a king, but now you have to obey me," Patches grumbled. "Don't help."

"Right," Elliot said. "Sorry."

This time he relaxed his body and did nothing to free himself, no matter how hard Patches groaned to pull him out. Even when it was only his toes remaining in the mud, he still let her drag him forward until he was entirely on solid ground.

"No one can get out of gripping mud on their own," Patches said between breaths. "Sometimes the Brownies call it friendship mud. If you don't have any friends, you stay stuck."

"Thanks for being my friend," Elliot said. "You saved me."

111

"You're welcome, but don't hug me," she said. "You're dirty."

Elliot heard a river nearby. "Give me a minute, and I'll be back." He ran to the river, this time being more careful to watch for any signs of gripping mud, then waded in. The water was cool but clean, and he splashed around until all the mud had washed away.

When he got back to Patches, she had caught her breath and was gathering up what little remained from his and Mr. Willimaker's food bundles. "Don't try to hug me now either," she said. "You're all wet."

"That gripping mud is pretty nasty stuff," Elliot said. "Is there a lot of it in the Underworld?"

"No, but you see it from time to time. You can sometimes see a brown glow around it. That's how you know it's there before you run into it."

"So why'd you come?" Elliot asked. "It's dangerous out here."

"I know," Patches said. "But I remembered a few things after you left. Some really important things."

"Like what?"

"Well, I wanted to tell you about the Shapeshifter in case he comes back and tries to trick you again."

Elliot shook his head. "He's on the surface, pretending to be me. That'll keep him busy until I get home."

"But if he does come," she said, "there's a way to keep him from changing forms. Just pinch his ear."

Elliot pinched two fingers against his own ear. "Like this?"

"The tighter, the better."

"Anything else?" Elliot asked.

"Yes. I'm worried about your helping the Pixies. I was thinking about a treaty the Brownies have. A really long time ago, Queen Bipsy agreed not to help either the Fairies or the Pixies while they were fighting over Glimmering Forest. I think the Fairies are going to be mad if they find out."

Elliot nodded. "Your dad told me the same thing last night."

Patches looked around. "Where is he?"

"The Fairies got mad," Elliot said. "They just took him."

Patches groaned. "My mom won't like that. After the Goblins took me, she made it a family rule that nobody else can get kidnapped."

"I don't think it was your dad's choice," Elliot said.

"My mom won't see it that way. She'll think he's trying to get out of weeding the garden."

Elliot shook his head. "He's fine for now, but the Fairies left me a note that said to get him back, I need one of Kovol's socks for the Fairies. I have to get to Demon Territory, but your dad had the map. Do you know how to get there?"

"Of course," Patches said. "Let's go."

"I don't want you to take me there," Elliot said. "Just point me in the right direction."

Patches put her hands on her hips. "It's still a long way, Elliot, and without me you'll be lost. Do you want my help or not?"

"Fine," Elliot said. "Let's go."

He followed Patches across a wide field of tiny white flowers that made him sneeze. And every time he sneezed, it blew the flower apart into bits that created new flowers where they landed. By the time they left the field, there were hundreds more flowers than when he began. He followed her up a tall, sandy hill where with every footstep he slid almost as far down as where he began. Patches was lighter and climbed it much faster but waited for him while he heaved his way to the top.

"That wasn't much fun," he said once he arrived.

"Yeah, but going down makes the climb worth it." She turned and leapt into the air, landing on the soft sand and rolling the rest of the way down the long hill.

Elliot followed, laughing as he rolled until he got a mouthful of sand and wisely kept his mouth closed the rest of the way. Once he reached the bottom, he and Patches lay on the sand and laughed a little longer.

"My dad would've taken you around the hill instead of over it," Patches said. "Now aren't you glad I'm here?"

Elliot nodded. "You have to go home soon, though. You can't come into Demon Territory with me."

"Oh, I forgot," Patches said, sitting up. "That's the other thing I had to tell you!"

But she never got a chance to tell him because at the last moment—

Dear Reader, don't you hate it when a character is about to say something really important, but they never get a chance to say it, because they're interrupted by something else? Maybe someday you'll have something really important to say, such as, "Mom, did you know the house is on fire?" Even if someone tries to interrupt you, like your little brother asking for a drink of water, you should still tell your mother about the fire. Not only was it rude for your little brother to interrupt and you have to teach him good manners, but your mother will probably also want to use that glass of water for the fire.

In this case, Patches never got a chance to finish what she was going to say, because Harold the Shapeshifter poofed in right in front of Elliot. He was still in Elliot's form, and the only reason she could tell them apart was that Harold had a small patch of white hair on the back of his head.

It took Elliot a moment to realize that it was not a mirror that had suddenly poofed in, but it was actually Harold, who looked exactly like him.

Elliot tried to say hello, but Harold spoke first. "I'm very sorry to tell you this," he said to Elliot, "but you'll have to stay in the Underworld forever. I won't let you go home ever again."

Chapter
16

Where Ears Become Important

Except for the Pixie prison, Elliot quite liked the Underworld and thought if he ever did get home, he might want to return for a nice visit one day. But he didn't want to stay in the Underworld forever. For one thing, his family was on the surface, and he missed them. For another, Underworld creatures thought chocolate was about the worst thing since liver and onions. Elliot couldn't see himself living anywhere without chocolate.

And he didn't at all like Harold the Shapeshifter telling him he couldn't go home again.

Elliot dropped his bundle just as Harold was drawing in a large breath of air to change into something, probably a scary something. He grabbed Harold's ear and held on tight.

"Stop that!" Harold said. "I've got to change into something that can kill you."

"I'm sick of everyone in the Underworld trying to kill me lately," Elliot said. "So it's bad timing on your part. I'm not letting go."

Harold grabbed Elliot's shoulders and started kicking his shins. In turn, Elliot kicked him back, all the time keeping hold of Harold's ear.

"That really hurts," Harold said.

"It's my ear I'm pinching anyway," Elliot said. "You're just borrowing it."

"It's your ear, but it's on my body, and it hurts. Want to see what it's like?" With that, Harold grabbed Elliot's ear.

"Ow!" Elliot yelped. "You're pinching harder than I am." So he pinched Harold's ear harder. In return, Harold began stomping on his feet.

"You can't stomp on a king's foot," Patches said. She rolled up her sleeves and flung some magic toward Harold, who suddenly sank to the ground like all the bones had gone out of his body. Elliot, who had been holding tightly to Harold's ear, also dropped to the ground, but he knew he still had bones, because they cracked against a rock as he landed.

"What did you do to him?" Elliot asked.

"I just zapped his energy for a couple of seconds," Patches said. "An Elf taught me that trick a while ago."

"Cool." Elliot leaned in to Harold and asked, "So why do you want to kill me?"

"I'm in love," Harold said. "We Shapeshifters sometimes do crazy things when we're in love."

"That's stupid," Elliot said. "Who are you in love with? My sister, Wendy? Because I've got news for you. You're up there pretending to be me, so if you go and fall in love with your sister, that's just creepy."

"It's not your sister," Harold said, "though I must say it's been nice to eat real human food after all this time. I've eaten so much of her food, it's really surprised her. She says I've never been as nice to her as I have this week."

Elliot groaned and Harold continued, "But, no, the girl I love is that beautiful human Cami Wortson."

For a moment, Elliot's brain went numb. He thought his heart had just stopped beating and that he'd faint and fall back into the gripping mud and sink to the center of the earth. And that would be fine, because not him or anyone who looked like him was ever supposed to even like Cami, much less claim to love her!

"No," he finally said. "No, you can't love her, because she's out to destroy my life. Which means as long as you look like me, she's out to destroy your life too. And if she finds out that you like her, she'll use that as a weapon that may or may not involve her reaching down your throat and ripping out your guts and feeding them to a crocodile!"

Harold sat up on his elbows. "That seems a little extreme for the love of my life."

Elliot shuddered. "Cami Wortson is not the love of your life. You'd have an easier time loving a toad. Trust me."

"And she has a nice smile," Harold said. "I don't think toads can smile."

Elliot had to give him that. He'd never seen a toad smile either. "Okay, listen," he said. "I have to let go of your ear now, because this is getting really weird. But don't try to change into anything that's going to kill me, because Patches will just zap your energy again."

"I can really only do that once," Patches whispered to Elliot, but he shushed her and hoped Harold hadn't heard.

Harold sat up. "I won't change into anything that can kill you. But I can't let you return to the surface again either. I've decided to remain as you for the rest of your life."

Elliot shook his head. "No."

"Why not? For your information, I've been a very good Elliot Penster. I'm probably better at it than you are."

"You can't be me, because nobody else knows the combination to my piggy bank. I've got my whole life's savings in there, and you'll never get it, because you don't know the combination."

"I broke the safe with a hammer and used the money to buy Cami some flowers," Harold said.

"Oh." That had been Elliot's best argument. "But did you have to buy flowers? Why didn't you just go ahead and propose marriage?"

Harold's eyes lit up. "Do you think—"

"No!" Elliot cried. "Listen, I'm not going to be here much longer. I just have to get a couple of things from Kovol, and then I'm going home, so you'd better get back up there and make enemies with Cami again."

"You're going to make Kovol mad," Harold said.

"Not if I don't wake him up," Elliot said.

Harold chewed on his bottom lip for a minute and then said, "How about this? I can change into a large bird and fly you to the border of Demon Territory in just a few minutes. It'll save you days of travel."

"No, thanks," Patches said.

"Wait!" Elliot said to Patches. "I lost most of our food in the gripping mud, and I'd rather get this over with."

"You shouldn't trust a Shapeshifter," Patches said.

Elliot turned to Harold. "Are you only flying me there so that Kovol can kill me faster and then you can be me forever?"

"Yeah, pretty much," Harold said.

Elliot looked back at Patches. "See? There's no reason not to trust him. He's telling the truth."

"About wanting you gone."

"Yeah, but it's still the truth."

"Okay," Patches sighed. "Fine."

Harold stood and drew in a deep breath. As the air moved inside him, he stretched his arms out wide. They expanded and grew into wings covered with long, brown feathers. His legs thinned and grew talons where his toes would have been. Finally, his nose stretched into a sharp orange beak, and his hair became smooth white feathers that covered his eagle head.

Harold looked at Elliot and cawed to get on his back. Elliot climbed on, then turned to Patches. "Listen, he's going to take me all the way to Demon Territory. I want you to go back home. I'll come back with your father in another day or two."

"No, wait!" Patches said, but it was too late.

Elliot had already climbed onto Harold the Eagle's back. As Harold lifted off the ground, Patches leapt into the air and tried to grab hold of Harold's tail, but Harold shook her off and back to the ground.

"Hey!" Elliot looked down. Patches was standing and trying to yell at him, but they were already too far away for him to hear her. He knew she'd be angry about his leaving so fast, but at least she was okay.

The view of the Underworld from the air was better than anything Elliot could have imagined. He could easily see back to Burrowsville, which from here looked like it was made of small mounds in the ground that served as the Brownies' homes. Then he stopped himself. The Brownies' homes *were* small mounds in the ground. Far in the distance he could see the Glimmering Forest. He wondered if Mr. Willimaker was being held somewhere near there by the Fairies.

Elliot was pretty mad at the Fairies and still mad at the Pixies. He was mad at Harold too, for wanting to take over his life, even though Harold was doing him a big favor right now. Of course, Harold was only doing him the favor so that Elliot could get killed faster. Then Harold, pretending to be Elliot, could declare his love to Elliot's worst enemy.

On second thought, Elliot seemed to have a lot of enemies lately. If he included Tubs, Grissel, the Fairies, and the Pixies, Cami was only his second or third worst enemy.

Harold cawed again and aimed a wing ahead of them. Elliot looked down at what appeared to be a long, black hole. Although it was late in the morning, it looked blacker than midnight in that spot.

That was Demon Territory. Somewhere in the middle of the blackness was the worst Demon in the history of time. And Elliot had to take a hair from his head. And now, one of his socks too.

They neared the territory and Harold flew lower to the ground, preparing to land. By now, Elliot couldn't see Burrowsville anymore. He couldn't see anyplace he recognized. The thought occurred to him that even if he somehow survived in Demon Territory, how was he going to get back to Burrowsville again?

He put his mouth close to where he thought Harold's ear would be, if giant birds had ears. "Will you wait around to fly me home when I come out?"

Harold shook his head so roughly that a few feathers fell free. Elliot didn't blame him. He wouldn't want to wait around either.

They landed in a clearing not far from the entrance to Demon Territory. Elliot slid off Harold's back, and soon Harold changed into the human boy he'd talked to on the surface.

"Okay, listen," Elliot said. "I had time to think up there, and I'll make you a deal. If I don't come back, then it's okay with me if you want to live out the rest of my life. Just promise never to tell my parents. My parents can be old-fashioned, and hearing that their son is really a Shapeshifter named Harold—well, they'd have a hard time with that."

"Yes, I've noticed that human parents are very strange about Shapeshifters taking over their children's lives."

"They love me," Elliot said. "But as long as they think you're me, I guess they'll love you too."

Harold kicked at the ground. "Now, why did you have to go and be nice to me when I'm clearly trying to help you get killed?" His eyes narrowed. "But in a way, being nice only makes me feel guilty for wanting you killed. It's not at all nice to make someone feel guilty."

Elliot shoved his hands into his pockets. "I have to go in there now, with or without your help. So don't feel guilty. Just go back and be a good me. Be a better me. I wasn't very nice to my family before I left them."

"It'll be hard to be better than the Elliot Penster I know," Harold said, "but I'll try. I'll be the kind of boy Cambria Dawn Wortson can love in return."

That pretty much ruined the moment for Elliot. He rolled his eyes and said, "Don't get too comfortable, though, because I am planning on coming back."

Coming back? Crazy thing to say, considering he didn't even know how to get in there first.

Elliot started to walk off, then with a smile turned to look back at the Shapeshifter. "I bet you can't get me inside Demon Territory."

"Bet I—" Harold stopped. "You're trying to trick me, aren't you?"

"Who, me?" Elliot raised his hands to show his innocence. "I just think it'll be too hard for you to get me into Demon Territory. I bet you're not that clever."

"Bet I am," Harold said, walking up to Elliot. "And I know you're tricking me, but I don't care, because it just so happens that I want to take the bet. I'll show you just how clever I am."

Elliot turned to look at Harold, but Harold had changed again. He was now an Elf. Probably. Based upon the Elves Elliot had seen in a lot of movies, Harold was not how he figured Elves would look.

Elliot had always thought Elves would be smaller than him,

like most Underworld creatures seemed to be. But Harold was tall, very slim, and very handsome. He had pointed ears on the side of his head, and his skin was pale in color.

"You're an Elf now?" Elliot asked.

"Elves are the caretakers of Demon Territory," Harold said. "No humans can get through."

"That's fine for you, but how do I get in?" Elliot asked.

Harold sighed. "Do I have to do everything? Honestly, you'd think I was the only one who wanted to see you killed today." He rubbed his hands together, then ran them along the edges of Elliot's ears. Elliot felt a tickling sensation in his head. When Harold removed his hands, Elliot touched his ears. They were pointed, like Harold's.

"You can change my shape?" he asked.

"I can only change a few small things, and those won't last more than five or ten minutes, so we've got to hurry. Are you ready for this, Elliot? Because after the next step you take, it'll be too late to turn back."

Elliot held his breath, closed his eyes, and took the next step.

Chapter 17

Where Elliot Has
an Embarrassing Secret

Harold and Elliot hurried to the entrance of Demon Territory, which was very clearly marked with a large sign, just as Fudd had described to Elliot. The sign said, WARNING: YOU ARE NOW ENTERING DEMON TERRITORY. ALL CREATURES MUST ENTER AT THEIR OWN RISK. HUMANS MAY NOT ENTER FOR ANY REASON.

Dear Reader, it's important to pay attention to signs. For example, if you ever see a sign telling you not to swim because there are alligators in the water, then you should definitely obey the sign. Sometimes alligators will pretend to be friendly, hoping to trick you into coming into the water. Then they'll eat you. However, if you ever see a sign telling you that it's okay to swim in a place where you know alligators live, you still shouldn't go in. It's possible that the alligators got a marker and changed the sign. Alligators are a lot trickier than most people think.

A female Elf as tall as Harold the Elf, but with long, golden hair, stood in front of the sign. Elliot thought she looked very bored. There probably weren't many creatures who came this way, so she probably didn't have much to do.

She straightened up as Harold and Elliot came closer. "You wish to enter Demon Territory?"

"We're on a long trip, and it's a shortcut," Harold said.

"I don't recognize you, Elf," she said. "What is your name?"

"We're southern hemisphere Elves," Harold answered. "We're here on a journey of discovery."

"Demon Territory is dangerous, even to Elves," she said. "I suggest you take the longer path."

"This is our path," Harold said. "You have no right to stop us, so allow us to pass."

"It's true I have no right to stop you," the Elf said. "I can only stop humans."

Elliot laughed like that was ridiculous. "Humans down here?" he said, slapping at his leg. "What is the Underworld coming to?"

The Elf looked at Elliot. "You don't look like an Elf to me."

"He's a young one," Harold said. "And notice the long legs. The rest of him will grow soon."

"No, it's in the face. It doesn't have the smooth beauty of Elfish skin. The eyes, there's too much fear in them for an Elf."

Elliot tried to get rid of the fear in his eyes, but that's not as easy as it sounds. The harder he tried, the more afraid he got that he couldn't get rid of the fear.

"Of course I'm an Elf," he said, then his eyes widened. "In fact, I'm so much an Elf that it's the initials of my name."

"Oh? What's your name?"

Elliot looked around. Suddenly he didn't want to say his full name. Not with Harold listening anyway. He leaned in close to the Elf female and whispered, "Elliot Louise Penster."

Dear Reader, clever as you are, you no doubt picked up on Elliot's middle name: Louise. And, yes, it is a girl's name. Here's how it happened. When Elliot was born, his middle name was supposed to be Louis. He would be named after his grandfather, Louis Penster, who was a war hero, a fighter pilot, and, lately, the slowest driver in the fast lane of the highway. The nurse who wrote down Elliot's name was very smart at nursing, but she was a terrible speller. This is because as a child, she played nurse on her dolls when she was supposed to be studying her spelling words. So when she wrote the birth certificate, she put an *e* on the end of Elliot's middle name, thus making him Elliot Louise Penster for life. His parents were saving up the money to get his birth certificate changed, but the money always seemed to go to other needs, like dinner.

"Elliot Louise Penster?" the Elf said. "Your initials spell ELP." (Apparently, the Elf was better at spelling than Elliot's nurse.) "And it sounds like a human name."

Elliot laughed. "Human name, yes, my parents—who are Elves, of course—are big fans of humans. In fact, that's the rest of my name. Elliot Louise Penster Human. E-L-P-H. That spells Elph."

Elliot was very good at spelling. And you have to agree, Dear Reader, that sometimes he is a very good thinker.

"Elph," the Elf said. "Let me see your ears."

Elliot turned his head so that she could inspect his ears. She tugged on them and twisted them until he said, "Ouch." That was the second time today someone had pulled on his ears.

"Very well," the Elf said. "You may proceed through Demon Territory. I advise you to be careful and stay on the path."

"Of course," Harold said.

They walked past the sign, then Elliot turned back and asked the Elf, "By the way, can you tell me where Kovol is? We'll have an easier time avoiding him if we know where he is."

"When the air around you is so black that you cannot see your hand in front of your face, then you have found Kovol," she said.

"So stay away from the pitch black. Good advice." Elliot thanked her and then ran to catch up to Harold. "Thanks for coming with me. I feel a lot better not being here alone."

"You are alone, because I'm leaving," Harold said. "But I must admit, I feel a little bad about helping you get killed. That doesn't seem right somehow. If you do die in here, I'll never be able to look at my face in the mirror again, which, of course, will be your face. Listen, I hate to do this, because I really love Cami, but I'm going to help you."

"You're coming with me to find Kovol?" Elliot asked.

"No way. I feel bad, but I'm not stupid." Harold withdrew a small bottle from his pocket. "This is some of that invisibility potion from my—I mean you and Cami's science fair project. I snuck it away because I wanted to test it when nobody else was around. You can rub this on you. It'll make you invisible while you pass through Demon Territory. You could move right past a Shadow Man, and he wouldn't even know it."

Elliot took the bottle. "How long does it last?"

"I don't know, but I tried some on myself and I stayed invisible until I shapeshifted again."

"Are you sure it works? Maybe you just shapeshifted yourself invisible."

Harold laughed. "I think I'd know if I were making myself invisible. Just use the potion, and if you hurry, you might get all the way to Kovol and out of Demon Territory before it wears off."

Elliot started to thank Harold, but he disappeared before Elliot got the words out. Elliot stared at the bottle, then put it in his back pocket. He decided to wait as long as possible before using it. It was still a little light here, so he doubted he'd run into any Shadow Men yet.

"Elliot?" Patches was in the middle of saying his name even as she poofed in front of him. She wrung her hands together, and her eyes darted around. She didn't seem to like where she was, but then, who would? (Other than evil Demon armies, of course.) "I'm glad I found you. It's very hard to poof in here, since it's so dark."

"Patches, I want you to go home," Elliot said. "It's dangerous here."

"If it's dangerous for me, then it's dangerous for you too."

"If your dad finds out I let you come with me to find Kovol, *he'll* be more dangerous to me than Kovol could ever be."

Patches frowned. "Yeah, that's probably true. But I tried to tell you something before you came here. I read a story a while back about why humans can't enter Demon Territory. The story said what keeps Kovol asleep is an agreement that no human will ever disturb the peace of his territory." Her eyes widened. "Elliot, I think you're disturbing the peace of his territory!"

Elliot paused a moment, then whispered. "Is the story fiction or nonfiction?"

Patches wound up her face. "Which is which?"

Elliot shrugged. "Can't remember. I thought you'd know. Was the story about Kovol sleeping a real one or made up?"

"I don't know. But what if it's real, Elliot? What if you've already woken him up?"

Once, Elliot had woken up Reed for breakfast without knowing he had already been up all night on a double shift at the Quack Shack. Reed had said a few words that would've made their mother's ears melt, then threw his Quack Shack cap at Elliot. Elliot had been more careful about waking up sleeping people since then.

Waking up evil Demons was probably worse.

Elliot put his hand on Agatha's flashlight and forced a smile onto his face. "I don't think the story is real. But even if it is, I'm not disturbing his peace. Just getting what I need and leaving."

Patches wrapped her arms around Elliot's waist. "You're the best king the Brownies have ever had," she whispered. "Hurry and get the hair and the sock, then get out."

"I will," Elliot said. "Now go home and be safe." Patches poofed away as Elliot took his next step deeper into Demon Territory.

He was certain it was already getting darker.

Where Elliot Tests
the Invisibility Potion

Near the Philippine Islands is an underwater canyon known as the Mariana Trench, which goes down almost seven miles beneath the surface of the ocean. It's deeper there than Mount Everest is tall. Light can't break through all the water to reach the bottom, so if you want to ask how dark it is, the answer, in scientific terms, is "super dark."

Elliot has never been to the bottom of the Mariana Trench (which is probably good, since the pressure of being in water that deep would crush him like a bulldozer running over a soda can). But Elliot didn't need to go to the Mariana Trench to understand true darkness.

All he had to do is look at the trail leading deeper into Demon Territory. Even from where he stood, the air was so dark he couldn't see the colors of things anymore. Everything around him was in shades of gray and brown. Or maybe everything in Demon Territory really was gray and brown. It would be silly to call it Demon Territory if it were all happy pastels.

But the trail narrowed ahead and looked like the kind of darkness where he could put his hand in front of his face and, if he was lucky, maybe see his fingers. But Elliot didn't care too much about seeing his fingers. His fingers weren't going to try to kill him.

The Shadow Men might. And they were somewhere ahead of him on the trail.

Elliot felt for the bottle of invisibility potion Harold had given him. It was still in his back pocket. How dumb, he thought, snorting in the air. Invisibility potion. What a stupid idea for a science project. If there was a potion that could turn people invisible, some company would already be selling it for fifty dollars a bottle.

Or maybe nobody knew about the potion yet. Harold said he had tried it and that it had worked on him. Maybe Elliot could sell it and make fifty dollars a bottle. Or more likely, Harold had accidentally turned himself invisible just because he wanted Cami's project to work.

Either way, Elliot wasn't going to use it on himself yet. Not until he had to.

He wondered again what his family was doing right now. Uncle Rufus hadn't stolen anything since he'd met Agatha. But had anything shiny caught his eye since Elliot had been gone? Had Reed gotten any more pickle relish from the Quack Shack? Whatever Wendy was burning for dinner tonight, Harold got to eat it, not him.

Sometimes when Kyle and Cole were flooding things, Wendy was burning things, and Uncle Rufus was stealing things, Elliot had wondered what it'd be like to live with another, more normal family.

He'd only been gone a few days, and yet he missed them— flooded, burned, stolen things, and all. Odd or not, they were his family.

It was time to finish this job and go home.

Elliot took several long steps forward, then stopped. The

sky had darkened. He felt for the flashlight at his side. *Not yet,* a voice inside him said.

Dear Reader, we all have a voice inside our head. It keeps us safe and helps us remember things we have to do. Usually when Elliot listens to the voice, he's very glad he did. You should listen to the voice inside your head too, unless the voice tells you to cut your sister's hair while she's asleep. If that happens, it might not be your own voice inside your head. Instead, it's probably an evil spell that a wizard put on you as his idea of a joke.

If you have an evil spell on you, dump all of your mother's salt on your bedroom floor, then stand on your head and kick your feet in the air. Your mother might be mad at first, but if you explain that you're just getting rid of an evil spell, she'll probably understand.

So Elliot walked deeper into Demon Territory, but after only a short distance, something changed. He heard a whisper in the air, a breath, a hiss.

Elliot looked at the tree beside him, with claw-like branches and long, spiny, gray leaves. The leaves were perfectly still. There was no wind here.

Then something moved on his right. Elliot's heart pounded. Cold sweat licked his palms. He had an itch in the middle of his back too, but that wasn't from fear. It just itched sometimes.

Elliot swung to his left at another sound. The trees beside him shivered as if something terrible was hiding there.

The Shadow Men had come.

With trembling fingers, Elliot grabbed the bottle of invisibility potion. That voice inside him said to test it on his finger first, but Elliot told the voice to be quiet. It was one thing for the voice to be sitting safely inside Elliot's head giving him orders, and a whole other thing for Elliot to be alone in Demon Territory with Shadow Men coming toward him.

Elliot pulled out the cork stopper and dumped the potion all over him. It tingled on his skin, like extra-fizzy soda pop. As quickly as he could, he rubbed it in, on his clothes, his skin, in his hair, everywhere but his eyes. For a brief moment he wondered if the potion would make his eyes go invisible, or if the Shadow Men would see nothing but a pair of eyes floating in midair. Maybe that would scare *them* for a change.

The tingling slowly faded, but the potion left his skin feeling greasy, even slippery. He didn't care. If Harold was right, he'd soon see himself start to become invisible, then he could slip right past the Shadow Men and get to Kovol.

Elliot raised a hand in front of his face. It was so dark, it was hard to tell whether he actually was fading, but he thought he could still see himself. Maybe that was how invisibility potions worked. Maybe he could always see himself, but nobody else could.

He decided to continue walking, conducting a little science experiment of his own. If the Shadow Men reached out and grabbed him in a few minutes, then, no, he was not invisible at all.

Experiments like this were why Elliot didn't like science projects.

There was more shuffling in the trees ahead. Something was definitely in there, watching, waiting for him to come closer.

Elliot walked a little farther, but he must have been moving away from Kovol now, because the area around Elliot seemed to be getting lighter, almost like he was carrying a soft yellow lamp.

Elliot was not carrying a soft yellow lamp. In fact, he wasn't carrying anything either soft or yellow. He had Agatha's flashlight strapped to his side like a sword, but it was turned off.

So what was causing the glow?

Elliot raised his hand in front of his face and gasped in horror. The invisibility potion was supposed to make him invisible, supposed to make it possible for him to slip past the Shadow Men without them being able to see him.

But somehow it had done just the opposite. The soft yellow glow was coming from him. Every part of his body that was covered in the potion was glowing. Elliot was the lantern!

And instead of being invisible to the Shadow Men, he was a beacon of light in the darkness. They could all find him now.

Chapter 19

Where Elliot Is Stuck Again

He was homesick, tired, and so scared that he could barely move a muscle. But mostly Elliot felt stupid. Harold probably did believe the potion would turn Elliot invisible. So even though Harold was trying to help, maybe that annoying voice inside Elliot's head was right. Elliot should have tested the potion on his finger before pouring the entire bottle all over himself.

Dumb voice, being right all the time.

There was nothing for Elliot to do now but run. He ran the way he used to when Tubs would chase him across Sprite's Hollow. No, he ran faster, the way he did that time he'd run from Cami when a game of kissing tag broke out during recess.

He was lightning. He was a cheetah. He was—Elliot

groaned as his foot landed in something familiar—he was stuck in gripping mud again.

Elliot struggled to pull his feet out, which only got him stuck deeper. Patches had told him before that he couldn't get out of gripping mud on his own. She was right all the time too.

Around him, Elliot saw the dark outlines of dozens of Shadow Men swarm in a circle around the gripping mud. He could feel the heat of their anger that he'd invaded their territory. Or maybe it really was heat. It was a warm night, after all, and he was beginning to sweat. They hissed at him and held out shadowy hands to pull him free. Yeah, they'd love to help him get out. Help him get out so they could finish him off.

These Shadow Men were far more frightening than the one Harold had turned into back at Sprite's Hollow. He could see into their eyes, or the empty holes that served as their eyes. They were without souls, just smoke and fire without light, whose only order was to serve Kovol. And serving Kovol meant killing any human who dared enter Kovol's territory.

Elliot braced himself for the worst. There was nothing he could do to fight them from here, and obviously his attempt at running away from them had failed. Would they get stuck in the gripping mud too? They didn't seem to touch the ground, so probably not.

They were trying to reach him, but Elliot noticed it didn't seem to be working. A Shadow Man would almost touch Elliot, but about the time he reached the glow on Elliot's skin, he'd stop and back off, then hiss in anger.

Elliot didn't like the hissing. It was different than a snake's hiss—which he didn't like too much either—but instead was a whispered screech. It made the hairs stand up on his arms and neck. Even in the warm night, goose bumps crawled down his spine.

They were angry. But they weren't coming any closer.

Another Shadow Man tried. He pushed just inside Elliot's glow with a shadowy hand, then Elliot noticed the hand disappeared. The Shadow Man yanked his hand back into the darkness with a different sort of hiss. This one was of panic, of pain.

Elliot raised his hand to his face again. He was putting off light. Light makes shadows disappear. Which means light makes Shadow Men disappear.

The glow from the invisibility potion may have called all the Shadow Men in Demon Territory to him, but as long as he glowed, they couldn't touch him. In a really strange way, he was safe.

Except, of course, that he was still sinking in gripping mud.

Someone needed to poof here to help him. Not Mr. Willimaker, who was currently locked in a Fairy prison. Not

Patches. She'd come if he called her, but Elliot refused to put her in danger.

The only one he could think of was Fudd.

But was Fudd working with the Fairies? Mr. Willimaker had thought there was a chance that Fudd was helping the Fairies stop Elliot. Then the Fairies had taken Mr. Willimaker away, leaving Elliot alone against Kovol. If Kovol succeeded in getting rid of him, Elliot had already asked Fudd to be the Brownie king.

Elliot didn't want to believe that Fudd was betraying him again. And lately everything about Fudd told him that the Brownie could be trusted. But if he was wrong, asking Fudd to help him get free of the gripping mud might be the very worst plan possible.

Elliot sank a little deeper into the gripping mud. Whether it was a good plan or not, it was his only choice.

Elliot cupped his hands around his mouth and yelled, "Fudd, I need you!"

The Shadow Men didn't like that. They began spinning in a circle around the mud. The air around Elliot thinned as the Shadow Men sucked it away from him. He wanted to call Fudd a second time but couldn't get a deep enough breath. He had to hope Fudd heard him the first time.

Elliot wanted to push his hand into the mud and find Agatha's flashlight. He could turn it on and chase all the

Shadow Men away. But he knew that once he put his hand in the mud, it would be stuck in there too.

"Fudd!" he called, more softly.

Although the Shadow Men were removing the air, if anything, the heat around Elliot was building. He wiped a bead of sweat off his forehead and then groaned as drips of light fell from his hand. Elliot was alone, surrounded by Shadow Men, stuck in gripping mud, and the one thing keeping the Shadow Men from reaching him was slowly sweating away.

Chapter 20

Where Fudd Gives an Order

Elliot was about to move to plan B in his hope of escaping the Shadow Men. Plan B was to cry like a baby and hope the Shadow Men became so embarrassed at being around him that they would decide he wasn't worth it. It wasn't a perfect plan, because Elliot knew that if he did it, he'd never be able to show his face in the Underworld again, but he was out of options.

And there was no plan C.

"Fudd," he breathed one last time.

"Your High—" Fudd said as he poofed in front of Elliot. His feet were at the very edge of the gripping mud, and he teetered forward as if he was about to fall in.

The Shadow Men advanced on Fudd, so Elliot stuck his arm as close to Fudd as he could reach, spreading barely enough light to protect him.

Fudd flapped his arms wildly to balance himself away from the mud, but it did no good, and he fell forward. A half second before he landed, however, he poofed himself away, poofing back almost instantly at a safer distance from the mud, though still within Elliot's light.

"My apologies for the delay," Fudd said. "It's very hard to find you in this darkness." He glanced back at the Shadow Men. "So this isn't going well."

"Stay as close to me as you can," Elliot said. "We're surrounded, but they can't touch me in this light. The more I sweat, the more the light is gone, though. I need your help to get out of here."

Fudd inched closer to Elliot. "I assume the gripping mud wasn't part of your plan."

"Of course not."

"Oh, good, because I couldn't help but think what a terrible plan that would have been. Like a rabbit hiding in the trap to escape the hunter."

"Just get me out of here!" Elliot scowled.

"Right away, Your Highness. Give me your hand." After a few grunts and several groans, Fudd pulled Elliot from the mud. Then he asked, "What do we do next?"

"Stay close and let me think," Elliot said. Warm mud dripped from his clothes, pulling the glowing potion off him with every drop.

Fudd didn't need to be reminded to stay close. He pushed so close to Elliot that there was no room for air between them.

Fudd tapped Elliot's shoulder to get his attention. "Back in Burrowsville, I've been reading about Kovol. Patches reminded me about the story with Kovol. She's right. Either Kovol is awake, or he soon will be."

"Kovol's awake?" Elliot shuddered. "That sounds bad."

Fudd shrugged. "If you think it'd be bad for the entire human race to collapse and be ruled by an army of the undead, then, yes, I suppose it is bad." He paused for a moment, then added, "I can help."

"I might not want any more of your help," Elliot said. "I'm not sure I can trust you."

Fudd looked at Elliot as if he'd been slapped. "Your Highness?"

"Mr. Willimaker is gone. The Fairies took him until I get Kovol's"—Elliot paused and wondered if the Shadow Men were listening—"until I do something for them too. Did the Fairies contact you?"

Fudd's eyes widened and he drew his hands together. "Can we talk about this when we're not surrounded by hundreds of creepy Demon servants?"

"Hundreds? Mr. Willimaker told me there'd only be fifty."

Fudd shook his head. "Based on the numbers here, I suspect there's closer to fifty thousand Shadow Men in Demon Territory."

A trickle of sweat rolled down Elliot's cheek. He wiped it free and saw the light so dim around his body that the Shadow Men could now get within inches of him. He began backing away with Fudd on his toes at every step.

"The flashlight," Elliot whispered.

"Not yet. It's for the darkest of dark places." Fudd's voice shook as he spoke. "I'm afraid there are darker places ahead of you."

"It's dark enough. I can't see where we're going."

"Your light is almost gone," Fudd said. "But I can't poof you away. My magic is too weak right now."

"Last night, Mr. Willimaker made a cold fire in his hand. Are you strong enough to do that?"

"Yes, but it's not enough light for the two of us." Fudd glanced up at Elliot. "The Fairies did ask for my help, but I told them no. After the Goblin war, when I said I'd never again betray you, I meant it. You are my king." Fudd flattened his palm, and instantly a spark of fire appeared on it. He placed it onto Elliot's hand, who thought it was surprisingly cool amid all the heat created by the Shadow Men. It gave off enough light to surround Elliot, but the light wasn't enough for Fudd. "This will only burn for a few minutes," Fudd said. "Run fast."

Elliot shook his head. "What about you? Make more fire."

"I can't. Not yet. I'll run in the other direction. Without a light, the Shadow Men will follow me instead of you. I'll run for as long as I can and then poof away."

"Don't get caught," Elliot said. "That's a king's order."

"There won't be much time, so don't you get caught either. That's a friend's order." After a short bow, Fudd poofed himself away. He must have reappeared at a close distance from the Shadow Men, because Elliot heard him yell, "Hey, Shadow Men! You can't catch Brownies or Goblins or Elves. You're so slow, you can't catch yourselves!"

Almost instantly the Shadow Men turned from Elliot and swarmed toward Fudd. Elliot took off in the direction where Demon Territory looked darkest, although he didn't dare run too fast. Not only was he afraid the breeze would blow out the small, cold flame that danced on his hand, but it also didn't throw light very far ahead of him. The last thing he needed was to run into more gripping mud.

He ran until his lungs ached and then ran until worry made his lungs do little flips in his chest (which can really hurt, if you think about it). Fudd had said he wouldn't be able to give Elliot a lot of time to get away. But it had been a long time and Elliot still hadn't seen any more Shadow Men. Did that mean Fudd hadn't been able to poof away before they caught him?

Elliot made a promise to himself. If he, Fudd, Mr. Willimaker, and, yes, even Tubs, made it out of this alive, Elliot would never enter Demon Territory again. Not even if they put up the best theme park ever and let him come for free. Not even if they had the fastest, tallest roller coaster and no long lines. But…what if they also gave free cotton candy?

Elliot shook that thought out of his head. Now was not the time to think about cotton candy. That soft, sticky, sweet, chewy sugar rush. It was a good thing he wasn't thinking about it, because otherwise he wouldn't have noticed that his fire had burned out. And that the air around him was so black, it would have even put out a firefly's light (if a firefly were stupid enough to come in here).

Elliot froze, not sure where he was or where he should go next. About the only thing he was sure of was that the snores he now heard could only be coming from the most evil tonsils in the Underworld.

Somehow, Elliot had found Kovol.

Chapter 21

Where the Flashlight Is Turned On

Kovol wasn't awake. Or at least Elliot was pretty sure he wasn't awake *yet*. He'd never heard anyone snore when they were awake, and that was definitely snoring.

He thought back to the night when all of this had started, when Tubs's snoring had kept Elliot awake half the night. He sort of wished he hadn't complained about that snoring, because this was much, much worse.

Elliot figured he must be in some kind of cave, because the air moved whenever Kovol breathed. When he snorted air in, a cold wind blew from behind Elliot's back toward Kovol. And when Kovol exhaled, the foulest smell rushed at Elliot's face, like rotting, decomposing eggs.

Demon morning breath.

So Kovol was asleep, but he seemed to be rolling around a lot, as if he was restless. As if he knew a human was in this cave with him. He could wake up at any second.

Elliot kept one hand by his flashlight, ready to flip it on as soon as he had to. He knew he'd have to use it soon, because he couldn't find a sock and a hair without it, not in this darkness. But he didn't want to turn it on too early and have the light wake up Kovol. He crept forward on tiptoes, testing every footstep before he put his full weight down. Snails moved faster than him, but he didn't care. He had only one chance at this.

With every step, he was closer to Kovol. He stopped every time the snoring stopped and it sounded as if Kovol rolled over. Then the snoring would begin again, and he'd continue forward. Once or twice it sounded as if Kovol had stopped breathing entirely for a second or two, but he always started again with his next snore.

Dear Reader, there is a condition known as sleep apnea in which a creature might stop breathing entirely for a second or two. This is not just for evil Demons. Several humans have it too. If you have this condition, you are lucky, because a doctor can treat it, and you'll be fine. Sadly, no doctor can help Kovol, mostly because Kovol would likely rip the doctor's arms off first. If you have a condition where you stop breathing for an hour or two rather than just a second or two, this is not sleep apnea. This means you're dead, and you should go see a doctor right away, even before you finish reading this book, no matter how exciting this chapter is.

After twenty steps, the snoring was so loud that Elliot was sure Kovol was within an arm's reach of him. He silently pulled out his flashlight and then put the lens inside his shirt so that when he turned it on, it would give off only dim light.

He flipped it on, then immediately turned the light toward his body. It was very bright. Bright like a miniature sun were inside it. Of course, Agatha had said it got its light from the sun. Elliot didn't understand how this flashlight worked, but magical tool design was hardly his biggest concern right now.

Even with the lens pressed against his skin, Elliot had enough light to see the dim outlines of Kovol's body. He was asleep but kept stretching and rolling over like he was trying to wake up. It must be hard to wake up when you've been asleep for a thousand years.

Kovol slept on a flat rock that seemed to have molded to his body while he slept. Like memory foam, but less comfortable. He was very tall, at least twice Elliot's height, maybe more. He was dressed with only a cloth around his waist and had leathery purple skin. His ears were long and pointed, and the horns on his head were gray, sharp, and twisted. His hands were gnarled with long fingers and fingernails that ended in spiked points. The skull of something that once might have been human was cuddled under his arm, like the Demon version of a teddy bear.

Elliot aimed the reflection of his light toward Kovol's feet. How could the Fairies possibly have wanted a sock? Anyone who looked like this, dressed like this, wasn't going to wear—oh, there they were. His socks.

Maybe sleeping in a cave for a thousand years gives a creature cold feet. Kovol's socks were long and thick, made of the skins of some animal Elliot didn't recognize.

Elliot stood as close as he dared to Kovol's feet and tried to ignore the stink that came from them. Maybe this was why his mother always told Elliot to sleep with his socks off, so he didn't have foot sweat at night.

Demon foot sweat was pretty awful. Like sticking your

head into a garbage can full of old, rotten fruit that's been baking in the sun for a week.

Elliot stuffed the flashlight into his pants so that he could free both hands. He put his fingers on the sock closest to him and very slowly rolled it down Kovol's meaty leg, then over his shin, then—Kovol yawned, a wide yawn that reeked of moldy fish, and he turned over. His movement trapped the sock Elliot had been unrolling under Kovol's other leg.

Elliot made a "why me?" gesture with his hands. He'd made it this far with more problems than anyone deserved. Couldn't he get a break for once?

He pinched the new sock between his fingers. This one was already resting at Kovol's ankle, so he decided to pull it off from the evil Demon's toes, like pulling off a glove.

He pulled very slowly, pausing every time Kovol twitched or stopped snoring. After what seemed like hours, Elliot finally pulled the last of the sock off his foot. Even while asleep, Kovol must not have liked the feel of only one sock, because he pushed the remaining sock off with his big Demon toe.

Elliot picked it up and put both socks in his pocket. That way, if he lost one he'd have a spare. Elliot took a deep breath. Halfway there. This wouldn't be so bad.

Then Elliot crept up to the top of Kovol's body, standing beside his head. The Demon yawned, revealing a long row of spiky teeth.

He tilted the flashlight just enough to see Kovol's head. All he needed was one hair, so he'd pull it, then get out.

But Elliot hadn't expected this.

There was no hair. Whatever Kovol had looked like when the Pixies last saw him, he was very different now. He was a bald Demon.

Elliot leaned in closer to Kovol. There was no hair on the rock slab, although the way Kovol created a wind with every snore, he'd probably scattered his fallen hair all over Demon Territory.

One hair, surely Kovol had one hair left.

Elliot needed a little more of the light from the flashlight, and he worried because Kovol's snoring had turned to softer breathing. The light probably bothered him.

There! Right on the center of his head. One long, coal black hair that had been lost in the shadows. One hair. That's all Kovol had left and all Elliot needed.

He rubbed his fingers together to get rid of any sweat on them and then pinched the hair between his thumb and forefinger. Elliot held his breath and closed his eyes tight as he plucked the hair.

He had it! Kovol's socks and Kovol's hair. Elliot shoved the hair into his pocket and then raised his arm again to steady the flashlight.

Only something grabbed his arm with a grip so tight that Elliot wondered if it would pinch his hand off.

Elliot looked up and found himself staring directly into eyes as black as the deepest darkness and full of anger that could only belong to something truly terrible.

Kovol was awake.

Chapter 22

Where Elliot Had Better Run Fast

Kovol yanked Elliot into the air, hanging him by his arm. He yelled out something in words Elliot couldn't understand. They probably weren't words at all, unless there's a word in Demon language that sounds like "Arrroooowwagh!"

If there is a word in Demon language that sounds like "Arrroooowwagh," then it probably means, "It's not polite to pull my hair out when I'm sleeping. Now I have to kill you."

Elliot screamed back at him. Not *at* him, really, because who'd be stupid enough to scream in a Demon's face? But Elliot did scream something that sounded like, "Waaahh," which, as all humans know, means, "I have to use the bathroom really bad."

The Demon dropped him to the ground and growled,

"What have you done?" His voice sounded like the roar of a rockslide down a mountain.

"I needed a hair," Elliot tried to explain. "For the Pixies."

Kovol ran his hand over his scalp. His eyes widened and went from shock to anger to rage. "You made me go bald, human."

"I only took one hair," Elliot said.

"And before you took it, I had hair. Now I'm bald."

If this had been a less serious moment, Elliot would have pictured Kovol in a wig. But it was a very serious moment, not the time for Demons in wigs.

"I'm sorry," Elliot said. "Please let me go."

Kovol laughed. Not in a funny, ha-ha sort of way, but in an evil, prepare-to-die sort of way. "No human goes free from Kovol. And because of you, I will now destroy every human on the face of this planet!"

Well, that's all Elliot needed. To be forever branded as the kid who got Earth destroyed. Who'd want to be his friend now?

"I'll start with you," Kovol said. "It will take a hundred years to fully finish you off, and I will enjoy every moment of it. Where to start? I think with your legs."

Elliot fell to his back. As Kovol reached for him, Elliot fumbled with the flashlight, pulled it out of his pants, and shone it directly into the evil Demon's eyes.

Kovol made a new scream this time. Not of anger or

revenge, but of pain. He clutched at his eyes and stumbled backward onto the stone slab.

Elliot scrambled to his feet and raced out of the cave. This time, with the help of the flashlight, he could see exactly where he was going. It was a good thing he hadn't seen the cave before. It was creepier than he had imagined, with moss and giant spider webs, and rats running along the sides of the walls. Something was hanging in a corner of the cave, but he didn't have time to figure out what. And there were bound to be snakes here too. Giant ones with ten heads that had big poisonous fangs.

Elliot heard Kovol running behind him. The Demon's feet shook the ground, and rocks tumbled to the ground beside Elliot with each of Kovol's steps. Elliot cleared the cave and paused briefly to decide which direction to run in to leave Demon Territory. Which way were the Shadow Men? Which way was the closest border?

As if he knew.

So he chose the easiest path, where there was a sort of trail between thorny bushes and dense, overgrown trees. Kovol crashed through the trees behind him and emitted a howl that Elliot instinctively knew was calling the Shadow Men to him.

Elliot kept running. His heart pounded so fiercely inside him that he could barely breathe, but as he found out, you don't really have to breathe to run, not if you're running to keep from having your legs ripped off.

The air warmed around Elliot, which normally he would have thought was because he was running so fast. But this was hardly a normal time, so he knew it was warming because the Shadow Men were getting closer. In the light from the flashlight he saw smoke rising like black vapor from their bodies. They were coming to serve Kovol. They were coming for Elliot.

It sounded like the Shadow Men were coming from the right, so Elliot darted to the left. He almost darted into an area with a brown glow hanging over it, but this time he stopped himself, barely avoiding landing in the very same patch of gripping mud where he had fallen last time.

Elliot tiptoed around the gripping mud, but he had to hurry. With the flashlight on, it was easy for both Kovol and his army to know where Elliot was. He had to get away.

Or did he?

A plan formed in Elliot's mind. It was dangerous, and his mother would have killed him if she had known what he was about to try. But not getting killed was the whole idea of his plan.

"Help!" Elliot cried. It wasn't hard to make his voice sound panicked. Even with a plan in mind, he was still in a pretty good panic.

Somewhere behind him, Kovol adjusted his path to run more directly toward Elliot. He heard Kovol's laugh as he sent another howl into the air. Elliot could feel the Shadow Men getting closer. He hoped Kovol would reach him first.

He crouched low in some thick, prickly weeds beside the patch of gripping mud. Within seconds, Kovol crashed through, and just as Elliot had almost done, Kovol ran straight into the gripping mud.

Kovol thrashed around violently, which of course made him stuck even worse. Elliot shook his head. When Kovol had time to think about this moment later on—and Elliot intended to make sure he had a long time to think about it later on—he was going to feel pretty stupid about the thrashing.

Elliot stuck the handle of the flashlight into the dirt, too far away for Kovol to reach it, but at such an angle that it threw light all around the Demon's body.

The Shadow Men swarmed in to the sound of Kovol's angry screeches. They seemed to have forgotten all about Elliot. They kept trying to push into the light to reach their master, but each time any part of the light touched them, they vanished within it. They hissed in anger and frustration. Trapped inside the mud, Kovol gnashed his teeth and cursed his army for their failures.

Kovol turned to Elliot. In a voice that was so calm it sent a chill up Elliot's spine, he said, "One day a solar eclipse will put out that flashlight. When it does, my army will free me. Watch for me that night, human, because I will come for you and destroy everything. You will regret the day you awoke me."

If Elliot had any ability to speak right then, he might have told Kovol that he already regretted this day. But it seemed a little too late for apologies. Kovol didn't seem like the forgiving type.

So he pushed out his chest and forced himself to sound brave as he said, "I'll be ready for you, Kovol. If you're smart, when you get out of this gripping mud you'll just go back to sleep. I've defeated you once, and I can do it again."

He wasn't sure that was true, but he liked the way it sounded. And it really made Kovol angry. Kovol began slapping at the gripping mud again, trying to reach Elliot.

Elliot stood as far from Kovol as he dared, but as close to the flashlight as he could. Here was an interesting problem. As soon as he left the light, the Shadow Men would get him. In trapping Kovol, he'd trapped himself.

Chapter 23

Where Elliot Likes Eagles

Elliot was in the middle of what he called half of a perfect plan. This must be why his father always said to never do a job halfway. Although Kovol was stuck and the Shadow Men couldn't reach him, Elliot was stuck too.

Above Elliot came a familiar squawk. He looked up and his eyes went as wide as manhole covers (well, almost as wide. Eyes can only stretch so far). "Harold!"

Harold the Eagle circled in the air over Elliot. The Shadow Men leapt up, trying to reach him, but Harold could always fly higher than they could leap.

"Your Highness!" Fudd called from Harold's back. "We're here to rescue you! Hold out your arms."

Elliot obeyed. Immediately Harold soared down, moving faster than the Shadow Men had time to react, darting between them like a fly that can't be swatted. He picked up Elliot with a giant talon and yanked him back into the air.

As they lifted off, a Shadow Man leaped forward and grabbed hold of Elliot's leg. Elliot felt the burn of his grip and yelled, but he could not shake him off.

"I'll save you, sir!" Fudd jumped off Harold's back and landed on the Shadow Man, holding him by the shoulders. The Shadow Man hissed and spat something into Fudd's eyes. Fudd reared back, yelping in pain. In his flailing around, Fudd kicked the Shadow Man, who released Elliot's leg. Both the Shadow Man and Fudd started to fall, but Elliot grabbed Fudd by the back of his pants, and Harold lifted them higher into the air.

The Shadow Man tumbled to the ground, landing in a burst of smoke and flame. Other Shadow Men hovered beneath them as they flew, hoping for a chance at Fudd or Elliot.

"I can't see!" Fudd cried. "He blinded me."

"You'll be okay," Elliot said, although he wasn't sure that was true.

"Let me go," Fudd said. "I'm slowing you down!"

"Just stop wiggling," Elliot said. "I can hold you."

Harold cawed that he was flying as fast as he could. And he was flying really fast. Elliot wasn't sure how he knew which way to go, because even up here Demon Territory was very, very dark.

Slowly, the Underworld light began to get brighter like an airplane moving down through clouds to reveal the city below. There are no clouds in the Underworld, Dear Reader, and certainly no airplanes, but you probably get the idea.

Soft pastel light filled the horizon in front of Elliot, a sunrise that could only happen in a mythological world. He described it to Fudd, who said, "It's the last painting of the Star Dancers each night. How I shall miss seeing it."

Every color of the rainbow found its way into the morning light, except pastel black, because there's no such thing. It was warm in a comforting sort of way, and Elliot felt his body relax just to cross into it.

He'd been in Demon Territory all night. In a place that never saw sun and never felt any sort of warmth that didn't burn.

Harold paused on the ground long enough for both Fudd and Elliot to climb onto his back, and then Elliot ordered Harold to take them directly to Glimmering Woods.

"Wouldn't you rather go to Burrowsville and rest first?" Fudd asked. "We've made you some new clothes. Better clothes."

The clothes Elliot wore were now muddy, burned, and soaked in sweat. He didn't mind that he had ruined them. It saved him the trouble of telling the Brownies there was no way he could wear them back to his home.

"Patches can bring the clothes to Glimmering Woods," Elliot said. "I want to see what can be done about your injury. And I want to get Tubs and Mr. Willimaker back."

"Don't worry about me," Fudd said. "But, Your Highness, I'm concerned about you giving the hair and sock to the Pixies and Fairies. We've had a treaty agreeing to stay out of their battle for the Glimmering Woods. Whatever you do may change that."

"That's okay," Elliot said. "I have a plan for that too." Then he asked, "When did Harold come back from the surface world?"

"When I ran from the Shadow Men, they were a little slow to follow, because it was really you they wanted. But they couldn't get you with the light, so they finally came for me. I ran and ran and bumped straight into Harold. He came back to tell you that he had tested the invisibility potion again and not to use it. So I bet Harold that he couldn't save both me and you without getting caught by the Shadow Men."

Elliot laughed and patted Harold on what he thought was an eagle's shoulder. "You took this bet. What did you win?"

Harold shrieked, then said, "I get full rights to your life whenever you're not using it anymore."

Elliot smiled. "Okay, but for the record, I can hardly wait to get back to my life. You'll have a while to wait."

Harold did whatever an eagle would do if it could shrug. Elliot lay on his back as they flew and just closed his eyes for a little rest.

Where the Fairies and Pixies Find
Something They Can Agree On

It didn't take long after Elliot arrived in Glimmering Woods for the Fairies to gather. It would take the Pixies longer, Harold explained. They were doing their hair.

Elliot hadn't really met the Fairies before. They hadn't bothered to say hi while they were stealing Mr. Willimaker.

They looked young, but not childish the way Pixies did. They were very beautiful, with flawless skin and elegant pastel clothes. They were a little larger than the Pixies and could also fly, although they had no wings.

A female Fairy flew up to Elliot and introduced herself as Aphid Flutterby. It was too bad he couldn't tell his brother Reed about the Fairies, because he would instantly fall in love with her long, coal-black hair and eyes as bright as a summer sky. "So, like, we have no royalty," Aphid said. "But I can totally speak for the Fairies."

Elliot smiled. "You speak like Fidget."

Aphid's mouth dropped open. "Fidget Spitfly, the Pixie princess? Like, gag me! I so totally don't. I speak like the humans on the totally awesomest show ever, *Surfer Teen*. Do you know the show?"

"I so totally do," Elliot said.

This seemed to make Aphid happy. "Do you have the sock?"

"Do you have Mr. Willimaker?"

Aphid nodded. "Totally. He's been chilling with us. If you ever want to enjoy captivity, Fairies are way nicer than those lame Pixies."

"I'll keep that in mind," Elliot said. "Now I want to see him."

Aphid nodded her head, and in a flash of light Mr. Willimaker appeared beside them. He fell to his knees and with tears in his eyes said, "King Elliot, I thought I'd never see you again. And no offense, but you look awful."

Elliot could hardly be offended at that. He knew how bad he looked.

"Like, you couldn't have come back at a worse time," a voice behind Elliot said. He turned and saw Fidget fluttering in the air behind him. "I was totally about to get my nails done." Then Fidget pointed at the Fairies. "What are *they* doing here?"

"Since you forced the human to help you, we decided to do the same," Aphid said, cocking her head in anger.

"That's so not awesome," Fidget scowled. "My daddy is going to be totally mad at me!" She turned to Elliot. "So did you get the hair or not?"

"And we want the sock," Aphid demanded.

"Where's Tubs?" Elliot asked.

Fidget groaned. "Like, give me the hair, and I'll return him to the surface. We're totally tired of him anyway. He never stops eating. I'm so grossed out."

"You have to return him with no memory of the Underworld," Elliot said.

"Duh! Do you think we want a grody human like that knowing about us? When he goes back, he won't remember any of this. Now, where's the hair?"

"Where's the sock?" Aphid said.

Elliot pulled a sock from each pocket.

"Two of them?" Aphid said, eyeing Fidget. "That's so awesome! Twice the power against Pixies."

"I can smell them from here," Fidget said. "They're, like, totally gagging me. You'd better have gotten two hairs then."

"Kovol had only one left," Elliot said. "But watch this." He pulled the hair from his pocket and tore it in half. Fidget's smile of triumph quickly faded as Elliot stuffed one hair in each sock. Then he held them out to Aphid and Fidget.

"I am so not touching that sock," Fidget said. "Even to get the hair."

"It's making me gag," Aphid said. "I totally won't take the sock as long as it has a hair inside."

"Suit yourselves," Elliot said, laying the socks on the ground. "But I did what you each told me I had to do to get Tubs and Mr. Willimaker back. The Fairies have their sock, and the Pixies have their hair. It's not my problem if you don't want them now. But you have to keep your promises."

Fidget stamped her foot. "What-ever. " She waved her wand and then with a glare at Elliot said, "Pixies don't like to be tricked. Anyway, that human, Tubs, is home now. If there's any good news, it's that he's out of my hair. My beautiful, beautiful hair."

"The Fairies don't like to be tricked either," Aphid said. "And for the record, we have way better hair. But all we really wanted was to stop the Pixies, so at least after all this, nothing has changed."

"Actually, a lot has changed," Elliot said. "What you did got me to wake up Kovol, which means the entire Underworld will have to defend against him one day. My friend Fudd Fartwick was blinded in saving me from the Shadow Men. And I used to think Pixies and Fairies were pretty cool, but I don't think so anymore. If you want the Brownies to help you when Kovol does attack the Underworld, you'd better start being a lot nicer to me."

Aphid and Fidget glared at each other. "Gag me," Aphid said at the same time as Fidget said, "Totally gross." Then their eyes widened and they looked back at each other.

"*Surfer Teen?*" Fidget said.

"*Awesomest kid on the scene?*" Aphid added.

The Pixie and Fairy squealed in some high pitch that probably caused a lot of dogs on the surface world to howl.

"So whatever about the war, that's so my dad's thing anyway," Fidget said. "We can at least hang out to watch the show, right?"

Aphid nodded, then turned to Elliot. "Like, I totally thought you'd be killed in Demon Territory, human. No creature has ever come back from there. So I guess when Kovol attacks the Underworld, the Fairies will fight with you in battle."

"The Pixies too," Fidget said softly. "You were awesome. Totally."

"And you saved my dad," Patches said. Elliot wondered how long she'd been there. She handed Elliot some clothes. "I helped our tailor with the design. I think you'll like them."

"We'll take care of Fudd," Mr. Willimaker said.

"Can you fix his eyes?" Elliot asked.

Fudd shook his head. "We don't have that kind of magic or medicine. But you shouldn't worry about me. I'll be fine."

"And I'll be there to help you." Mr. Willimaker clapped a hand on Fudd's shoulder. "Sorry I lost trust in you, old friend."

Fudd smiled. "We're friends? But I don't even know your first name."

Minutes later, Elliot had cleaned up and changed into a T-shirt and brown cotton pants. The pants were a little goofy, but at least they were from the right century. He wasn't sure about the T-shirt, which read, BROWNIES ARE FOR HUGGING, NOT EATING, but it would have to do until he got home.

Harold had changed back into an Elf to say good-bye to Elliot. "I admit that I'm not totally sad you survived and get to go home," he said. "On the one hand, there's Cami and she's wonderful, but on the other hand, Kyle and Cole are very naughty twins. They dumped a big bucket of ice water on me yesterday while I was outside talking to her."

Elliot chuckled. "Yeah, they do things like that. I never thought I'd miss it."

"So your science project is due today," Harold said. "I've done your share of the work for it. The problem is that Cami never found anyone willing to test it, so she's not sure if it works."

"It doesn't," Elliot said. "I lit up like a glow stick."

"I know. But I couldn't tell her I'd tried it on myself.

Obviously I made myself go invisible just to let her be right about the experiment."

"Will I see you around?" Elliot asked.

"I guess if you ever see yourself walking down the street, it's probably me."

"Don't do that," Elliot said. "One of me on the surface gets into plenty of trouble. Two of me would be too much."

"Hmm, we'll see." Harold changed himself to a sparrow. He began to fly away, then fluttered back and tweeted, "By the way, I'm really sorry about your bed."

"What about my bed?" Elliot asked, but it was too late. Harold was gone.

Chapter 25

Where Fidget Does Elliot a Favor

Elliot wasn't sure what things would be like when the Pixies poofed him home. He'd been gone for days. He'd been a prisoner to the Pixies and survived a Goblin's attempt to scare him to death. He'd been trapped in gripping mud—twice, fought off Shadow Men, and defeated Kovol. So it would make sense if things were a little crazy on the surface too.

However, his family didn't know about any of that. Tubs wouldn't even know it, since the Pixies had wiped Tubs's memory of the entire Underworld.

The last thing Fidget had said before she waved her wand to poof him away was, "Okay, so like, I'm sorry about the whole kidnapping thing. I know just how to make it up to you."

He didn't like the sound of that, but she poofed him away before he could ask what she meant.

He returned to the surface just outside his home. It was a cool, crisp autumn morning, and Elliot enjoyed the feeling of sun on his face. Although the Underworld had plenty of light, he had missed the sun. The large bucket of invisibility potion was nearby. It was bubbling more than ever, and Elliot was glad that at least it had not blown up his home while he was gone.

Strange, the things that made him happy ever since he had become king.

Harold had said the science project was due today. Did that mean Elliot had to somehow get the potion to school? His parents were probably already at work, so getting the potion there would be Cami's problem.

"Elli-ot!"

Elliot cringed. There was only one person who said his name that way. If getting the potion to school was Cami's problem, then Cami was his problem.

She began talking even before she rounded the corner to his backyard. "If we can't prove the potion works, then we're not going to get a good grade. So what—" She stopped and stared at Elliot. Her eyes widened, and then she let out a high-pitched scream like Aphid and Fidget had done. Why did girls always do that? More specifically, why was Cami screaming right now?

"Just wait there. I'll take a picture." The words tumbled out of her mouth so quickly, he wondered how she could pronounce them all.

"A picture of what?" he asked.

She began digging through her backpack. "Your legs, silly. I can't believe it worked!"

Elliot looked down at his legs. Or where his legs were supposed to be. He was standing on them, so he knew they still existed, but they were invisible. He sighed loudly enough for her to know he was bothered. This wasn't the potion. It was Fidget's way of making up for having kidnapped him.

"Don't fuss, it's just a photo," Cami said, finding the camera. "Now smile!" She snapped a picture, then said, "I guess you don't have to smile, because the photo is really just of your legs."

She took three or four other pictures and then gave Elliot a big hug (he promised himself to shower as soon as possible so that her girl germs didn't stick to him).

"I can't believe you tried the potion on yourself," she said. "Nobody else dared to do it. You are so brave."

Elliot wanted to say, "Well, I did battle an evil Demon." But all he did was shrug and wonder how long Fidget was going to keep his legs invisible. He didn't want to go to school like this.

As Cami put her camera into her backpack, she said, "You know, Elliot, I always thought you were a pretty cool kid, but I thought you hated me."

Elliot didn't know what to say to that. Calling her Toadface wasn't exactly a sign of burning love. But Cami continued, "Anyway, you've been extra nice to me these past few days, and I wanted to tell you thanks. Sometimes I feel a little out of place, and, well, it was just a good week."

Elliot frowned. He felt pretty bad now for calling her Toadface.

Cami put a hand on the potion. "So my mom's waiting out front in our car. I can get the potion to school, and I'll see you there, okay?"

"Are you sure you can carry that by yourself?" he asked.

She grinned at him. "Will you help me?"

Anyone who battled Demons and Shadow Men could surely defend himself against girl germs. Elliot went to the far side of the potion and after a "one—two—three" from Cami, they lifted it up.

"It's gotten heavier," Cami said. "Like it all turned to syrup or something."

It was heavy for Elliot too. He couldn't catch enough breath to say anything. They made it only four steps before Cami grunted a "wah," Elliot spat out a "whoa," and the entire bucket of invisibility potion tumbled to the ground. It spilled out like floodwater breaking free of the dam and quickly soaked into the dry autumn grass.

Cami and Elliot stood beside each other for several seconds. Cami made a small sniffling sound, and Elliot took a step away from her, certain she was going to cry floodwater tears as well.

But she didn't. She began laughing. Then she did start crying, but it was only from laughing so hard. "This is terrible," she said, still laughing. "What's going to happen to our grades now?"

"We still have the pictures on your camera," he said, laughing too. "And my legs."

"I can see your legs now," she said. "The potion probably splashed on them and turned them back."

He looked down and saw that she was right. Fidget had returned his legs to him. She probably had made the potion spill too, just so Cami couldn't try it on anyone else.

"Oh, well," Cami said, wiping a last happy tear from her eye. "We had fun doing the project, and I have the picture of your legs, so we'll get a good enough grade." She paused then added, "And I guess we're friends now, right?"

"Uh, right." Elliot scratched his chin, then said, "Hey, a few days ago when you were stuck in that mud my little brothers made, sorry I didn't help you get out."

"I finally made it out on my own," she said. "Good thing it wasn't quicksand."

"Or gripping mud," Elliot said under his breath.

He gave an awkward wave as Cami skipped out of his yard, calling back, "See you at school!"

"Look at this mess!" Wendy said, opening the back door to the house. "Elliot, what are you doing out here? I thought you left early for school."

"Nope. Just finishing up my science project," he said.

"Oh. Hey, that white patch in your hair is gone."

Elliot reached up to the back of his head. "Oh, yeah."

"I guess that bleach you spilled on it must have worn off or something."

Elliot didn't think bleach worked that way, but if Wendy believed it, he wasn't going to argue the point.

"Hey, did something happen with my bed?" he asked.

"Since you gave it to Tubs?" Wendy asked.

Elliot's jaw dropped. "I did *what?*"

"Don't you remember when Tubs's parents came to pick him up?"

Elliot's muscles tightened. "Obviously not."

"You told his parents he could stay for another night or two. They thought that was great, because he didn't have a bed, because he'd broken it last week. So you said Tubs could have your bed. We all thought it was really nice. Sort of strange, though."

"That is strange," Elliot agreed. "Doesn't sound like something I'd normally do." He planned to talk to Harold about that very soon.

"I think you did it to impress Cami," Wendy added. "Interesting clothes, by the way. Where did they come from?"

"A friend gave them to me."

"Oh." Wendy brushed some flour off her hands. "You might want to change into something more normal if you don't want Tubs to start beating you up again. Luckily, he's been really quiet these past few days, barely even moved off his chair in the corner. While you're changing clothes, I'll dish you up some breakfast. The eggs are a little burned, but the toast isn't too bad if I scrape it first." Then she frowned. "I know I'm not a good cook, Elliot, but I'm doing the best I can since Mom and Dad are so busy. So thanks for being really nice about it this week."

Elliot walked up to Wendy and wrapped his arms around

her waist for the best brother hug he could give. "Sorry I haven't been nice about it before this week. I'll be better. I don't know what our family would do without you."

"Our family wouldn't know what to do without you either," Wendy said, walking back into their home. "I mean, it's not like we could just go find another Elliot somewhere, right?"

Elliot smiled. Not if he could help it.

Acknowledgments

Thanks to Jeff, for every smile. The only one for me is you. Thanks also to Ron Peters, whose fine-tuned opinions are the first I look to for my writing, and to the late Tom Horner, whose sharp eye and unfailing encouragement I will miss. And to Ammi-Joan Paquette and Kelly Barrales-Saylor, for their valuable input and generous support of both this series and me.

And a final thanks to the old Elf who spent countless hours (18½ hours—I counted) unfolding to me the secrets of the Underworld. He literally would not stop unfolding things, even when I said I was late for dinner. Any inaccuracies about Pixies, Shapeshifters, or Demons is entirely my fault, namely due to the fact that I don't speak the Underworld language of Flibberish and thus had no clue what the Elf was talking about for all that time.

About the Author

JENNIFER A. NIELSEN lives at the base of a very tall mountain in Northern Utah with her husband, three children, and a naughty puppy. She loves fresh baked bread, campfires, and happy endings. Jennifer once saw an exact duplicate of herself in a store, so she was certain it was a mischievous Shapeshifter. Looking back on it now, she might have just been looking in a mirror. That would explain a lot, actually. Learn more at her website: www.jennielsen.com.

About the Illustrator

GIDEON KENDALL graduated from the Cooper Union for Science and Art with a BFA and has since been working as an artist, illustrator, animation designer, and musician in Brooklyn.